SYSTEMA PARADOXA

ACCOUNTS OF CRYPTOZOOLOGICAL IMPORT

VOLUME 10

FORGET ME NOT

A TALE OF BESSIE, THE LAKE ERIE MONSTER

AS ACCOUNTED BY CAROL GYZANDER

NEOPARADOXA

Pennsville, NJ

2022

PUBLISHED BY
NeoParadoxa
A division of eSpec Books
PO Box 242
Pennsville, NJ 08070
www.especbooks.com

ISBN: 978-1-949691-33-7
ISBN (ebook): 978-1-949691-32-0

Interior Design: Danielle McPhail
www.sidhenadaire.com

Cover Art: Jason Whitley
Cover Design: Mike and Danielle McPhail, McP Digital Graphics
Interior Illustration: Jason Whitley

Copyediting: Greg Schauer and John L. French

Dedication

To My Evil Twin

Chapter One

1969: Friday, June 6

Jane's heart raced as she stood at the top of the rickety dock ramp leading down to their friend's motorboat. The railing leaned in on the right, covered with peeling paint and thick spiderwebs. Moonlight reflected off the multifaceted eyes of the spider in the middle, the size of a quarter — or was it just her imagination?

"Good old North Buffalo Marina. Remember how much the spiders on the railings scared Mom when we came here as kids?" She looked over her shoulder at her twin brother, Rob. Both stood at the center of the dock ramp, as far away as possible from the two edges.

"I think Mom was on to something," Rob muttered. "I can't believe we're doing this after ten years of being safe on land."

Jane had a sudden image of all the swim lessons their father had tried to get them to do, all of which had ended with hysterics. She shrugged and squeezed his hand. Neither one made a move toward the water.

"Come on, guys!" George, a year ahead of them in high school and about to graduate, waved them down the ramp from the boat. "I've got it all set to go, and Marilyn's getting lonely, Rob. If you know what I mean."

He pretended to recoil in pain when the young woman in the green polka-dot bikini at his side swatted his elbow, then he grinned and held up a can of Utica Club beer. "Come on, man, get your ass down that ramp. It's a Friday in June, which means it's finally almost warm out. Gonna have some fun!"

Jane and Rob rolled their eyes, shrugged, and started slowly down the ramp. The blond sixteen-year-olds reached the floating dock at the bottom without mishap, but Rob grabbed her arm when the dock tilted under their weight. "Holy shit. Holy shit."

Jane linked arms with him and guided him toward the boat. "It's okay, come on. We've got this. It's not like we're six years old again. Nothing's gonna get us."

The two climbed over the side of the small wooden cabin cruiser. The leg of Jane's bellbottoms caught on a big splinter in the mahogany gunwale for a moment, making her heart lurch. As soon as she got untangled, she sat on the red vinyl bench seat in the open cockpit at the rear, holding firmly onto the boat's edge. Rob immediately went into the sitting area under the roof of the open cabin a few feet to the front.

Marilyn threw her arms around him in a big hug. "Hey, man! Took you long enough, but you made it."

He patted her shoulder and sank onto the bench seat on the left, opposite where George was at the wheel. "Yeah, we made it. It's gonna be fun. Right?"

George gave him a thumbs-up.

Rob's gaze flitted from the beautiful girl at his side to his sister. "Right? No sea monsters this trip." He laughed shakily.

George stepped off onto the floating dock to untie the boat, then leaped lightly back on board. The engine thrummed as he put it into reverse and backed carefully out of the slip, then negotiated them through the marina on the edge of the Niagara River by the growing light of the half-moon. Jane was glad it was a cloudless night so he could see where he was going.

When they were partway out into the current, he flicked on the running lights and grinned. "I mean, it's not really a problem that we're out in Dad's boat, or I liberated some beer from his fridge, but I don't feel the need to advertise to the marina folks, you know what I mean?"

He popped in an eight-track tape, and the sounds of The 5th Dimension singing *Aquarius* filled the boat.

Marilyn danced in the cabin, her hoop earrings swinging in time with the music and clearly visible under her pixie haircut. "Groovy song! Let the Sunshine! Ha-ha, at night!"

As the powerful little boat headed upriver, the waves picked up, and the boat bobbed up and down, proceeding through the chop. Jane pulled a red bandana out of her pocket and tied it over her long wavy blonde hair to keep it out of her face. Rob sat hunched with his arms gripping his knees.

Marilyn had trouble keeping her balance and sat down close to him. She leaned forward and touched his shoulder with hers, speaking loudly to be heard over the motor.

"So, what's the scoop? George told me that you've been scared of the water since you were a kid. Something happened?"

He snorted. "Yeah, you could say that. Jane and I were out in a boat with our parents, and some… something swamped the boat. Mom drowned."

Her eyes widened. "Oh, man, I didn't realize. I'm so sorry, Rob." She leaned her head on his shoulder. "So, you stayed away from the water ever since. Makes sense."

Jane listened from where she sat behind them in the open part of the boat. "And it wasn't just that. There was something in the water."

"*What?* What was in the water?" The young woman looked between the twins, eyes wide.

Rob shook his head. "I'd uh, rather not talk about it while we're out here in the boat if you don't mind."

George cut in. "Yeah, this is the first time I got them out here. Let's just have fun and help them relax, okay?" He reached into the cooler at his feet and pulled out a can of beer, passing it to Rob, who leaned forward and pulled the tab on his can.

"Jane?" Rob held it up toward his sister.

She shook her head. "No, thanks, I'm fine."

Marilyn reached over and grabbed the can, took a big gulp, and passed it back. "We can share, okay?"

He grinned and leaned back against the side wall of the cabin, turning partway toward his sister, and casually putting his arm across the back of the seat behind Marilyn—but holding onto the bench with his other hand in a white-knuckle grip.

George pointed the boat upriver. While it was late at night, there was a lot of light coming from shore—particularly the left side, where the buildings of Buffalo loomed taller and the lights brighter as they headed south from the northern outskirts toward the downtown section.

"Hey, Marilyn, so you just moved here? Where are you from?" Jane tried to distract herself from the queasy feeling she got from the boat pounding on the waves.

Marilyn's face lit up. "Yeah, we just came in from San Francisco because my dad got transferred. He works with George's dad. So now I have to finish up the last two years of high school in a new place. Seriously, I was kinda worried about not meeting people and being alone all summer. It was cool to find you guys."

"Well, I'm gonna graduate in a few weeks. I'll head off to college at Geneseo next year, but you guys'll all be seniors together!" George said.

She grabbed the beer can from Rob and raised it to click against George's can. "Cheers!" She took a big chug, then wrinkled her nose. "I love the water, but this is really different from the beach in California. Where exactly *are* we? And hey, far-out smell. Dead fish?"

George gestured ahead of them. "Lake Erie always stinks. Well, right now, we're on the Niagara River. See that bridge up there, all lit up? That's Peace Bridge. On our left is the US and on the right is Canada."

She leaned forward and looked ahead of them through the windshield. "Cool!"

"Yeah, on the other side of the bridge is Lake Erie. That's what you smell. It's not exactly clean water, shall we say?" George then pointed back over his shoulder with his thumb. "When we turn around to go back, we'll be heading toward Niagara Falls, and then the river dumps into Lake Ontario."

"Oh wow! So, that's why the current is so strong here? Because this heads over the Falls? I can't wait to see those!" As she turned and looked behind them, downriver, Marilyn leaned a little closer toward Rob, who casually put his hand on her shoulder.

George snickered a moment, then went on. "Yep, you got it. That's why I headed upriver, which is slower going against the current. After we go under the bridge into Lake Erie, the waves will get a little smaller, and we can just sort of hang out and enjoy the evening. It'll be a lot quicker to head back with the current."

She frowned. "So why can't I see Niagara Falls back behind us? I mean, I know it's dark and all."

Jane leaned forward. "It's about ten miles down. Plus, the Niagara River splits and goes around each side of a couple of islands by the Falls." At Marilyn's quizzical look, she went on. "Our dad's a hydrologist for the construction company that's building a dam to shut off the American Falls. He's working crazy hours, which is why we could sneak out here."

"What? Turn *off* Niagara Falls? You're joking." Marilyn grinned at Jane. "Uh, right?"

"Seriously, they're trying to stop the erosion of the Falls. They've been getting ready to dump rock in the river in a few days and turn it off, probably for months."

Marilyn's mouth dropped open. "Oh no! I need to see it first!"

"I can take you!" Jane said. "Maybe Sunday? Rob has to work then. Hey, do you watch *Dark Shadows*?"

Marilyn bounced on her seat a little bit. "Uh yeah, you know my last name is Collins, right? So yeah, I'm definitely gonna watch a soap opera all about the Collins family and their vampire. And, that Quentin is soooo dreamy!"

"Agreed!" Jane shivered a bit and rubbed her arms. "You know, Rob and I usually see this from land or the bridges, but I think I'm getting more comfortable with this boat idea. Even though it's like riding a bucking bronco."

Every time they surged into a wave, the front of the boat went up and then bashed down into the next oncoming wave, giving them a rollicking ride. Jane noticed the spray that rose from each descent and got brave—she stuck one hand over the edge to touch the droplets of water that sprayed up while still gripping tight to the gunwale with the other. The cold water made her fingers tingle and her heart soar.

After a bit, when nothing bad happened, she resolved to challenge herself more. Leaning farther over, she trailed her hand in the water, shivering.

"Jane, are you cold?" Rob pulled Marilyn closer to him, making room on the bench. "It's only June, after all. Wanna come up here where it's warmer?"

His sister grinned. "No, thanks, I'm trying to experience as much of this boat trip as I can stand. Marilyn, aren't *you* cold? I can't believe you're wearing a bathing suit at night in June. I mean, this *is* Buffalo."

"Hey, what do I know? In California, I'd already have a great tan!" Marilyn snuggled against Rob. "I guess you and your big blue eyes will just have to keep me warm."

Jane rolled her own blue eyes.

George pulled off his denim jacket, holding the steering wheel with his knee. "Here. Just be careful because my dad's car keys are in there." He passed it to Jane.

She snagged the jacket and wrapped it around her shoulders. "Thanks, man."

"You're doing great, ya know. I'm glad you made it out here." He turned halfway toward her and smiled.

"Yeah. Me too. I think."

As the Peace Bridge's colorful lights loomed nearer, Jane leaned against the bench, keeping a tight grip on the gunwale. She tilted her head back and watched the huge structure pass over them as George navigated through the middle archway. On the other side, she turned and watched the bridge get smaller, enjoying the reflections of the lights in the V-shaped wake left behind the boat.

As George had predicted, the waves got calmer. In a bit, he turned the motor down and let them enjoy the gentle water of Lake Erie on a calm night. With the boat more stable in the water and the engine quieter, they could hear the gentle lapping of the waves against the hull. The chemical smell of the polluted water invaded their nostrils even more strongly once there was less air blowing by.

"What do you think, man?" He nudged Rob's foot with his own as he pulled the eight-track before it could repeat. "Kinda nice, huh?"

"Yeah, I could almost get used to this." Rob finished his third beer. "Except for the stink."

George put on a Janis Joplin tape next. Jane let out a whoop, jumped up, and grabbed the empty beer can from her brother. She sang along with the first song, "Try (Just a Little Bit Harder)," using the can as a pretend microphone. Marilyn leaped up and joined in with background vocals.

When the song was over, Marilyn slid onto the bench next to Rob. He kissed her. She pulled back a moment and grinned at him. "Wow, and I thought 1967 was the Summer of Love!" She hopped onto his lap. After a moment, the two were fully occupied with kissing.

Jane carefully moved forward into the cabin area, grabbing ahold of the back of the driver's seat where George still kept one hand on the wheel. She tossed the can in the cooler and turned toward him, so her back was to the couple as she stood between the two seats.

"Oh yeah, much warmer under here. The breeze was pretty strong while we were underway. Thanks for the loan." She slipped his jacket off her shoulders and twirled it around like a bullfighter's cape to hang it over the back of his seat, still ignoring the couple making out.

He gave her a thumbs-up. "Looks like you're getting your sea legs. What do you think of the view from up here?"

"Cool. It looks different through the windshield. Kinda like being in a car." She looked out across the lake ahead of them. There were not many boats nearby, so she had a clear view of the water. After a minute, she leaned forward and peered intently.

"What?" George looked from her to the water. "See something interesting?"

"Well, it's weird. While we were underway, I noticed our boat left a V-shape in the water behind us. Kinda like that." She pointed through the windshield, where a ripple of waves approached the boat. "But what's making that wake? I don't see any boat."

George followed her indication and stared at the water. "Huh. I dunno. But it seems to be heading right at us. I think… maybe it's time to head home. Hold on."

He revved the engine and turned the boat in a half-circle toward the Peace Bridge. Rob and Marilyn came up for air, looking around to see what was going on.

The wind from the sudden acceleration blew the jeans jacket off the back of the driver's seat toward the side. It caught on the splinter in the gunwale that had snagged Jane's bellbottoms.

Jane dove at the jacket with a cry, landing on the bench and grabbing at the sleeve as the jacket fell halfway over the edge. "*No!*" She almost saved it from getting wet.

Almost. It was pulled into the water, trailing along the side of the boat.

George jumped up. "Jane! Be careful! Dammit, Rob, take the wheel." He charged across the boat, reaching her side just as she grabbed for the sleeve being pulled off the gunwale. "Dammit, my dad's gonna *kill* me!"

The two friends stared into the water as a dark shape dragged the jacket under the surface. A strong thump on the side shook the entire boat, and the water roiled in a continuous stream heading past the bow, toward the Peace Bridge.

And then it was gone.

"Holy shit! What the hell was that?" George sank back on the bench and wiped his face with his hand. "I mean, I know I had a coupla beers, but did you see that too?"

Jane was still gripping the gunwale with both hands. "Yeah… I don't quite know *what* I saw. But something took the jacket!"

"George? Hey, George! I don't know what I'm doing here," Rob called from the pilot's seat, gripping the wheel with both hands.

George headed back and took the wheel, leaving Jane looking over the gunwale by herself. She jumped as a dark shape broke the water's surface just ahead of the boat, then submerged again. "Look out!" As the boat veered to the side, she watched the spot and saw something just under the surface as they passed it.

Was that a pale eye watching her?

Chapter Two

Jane jumped away from the side, waving her arms to get her balance as she backpedaled away from what she thought she'd seen in the water. She turned to George and grabbed the driver's seat. "Okay, I don't know what that was, but I want to get out of here *now*. Let's go!"

"Going! Hold on." George revved the engine again, and the little cabin cruiser leaped ahead in the water, heading for the Peace Bridge. "It'll be quicker getting home, at least."

Rob reached behind Marilyn and clasped his sister's shoulder as she stood between the benches. "What happened? What did you see?"

She shook her head. "I have no clue. Something grabbed the jacket off the gunwale and moved past us. Then it turned around and came back by." She didn't mention seeing an eye under the water. She wasn't sure she wanted to admit to that — or even say it out loud.

Rob's fingers tightened on her arm. "Holy shit. Holy *shit*. Not again. Are you sure there was something there?"

"I… I think so. What do you think, George?"

The driver just shook his head. "No clue. But let me pay attention to getting us home. We can talk later after we get in the car. Oh shit. *The keys!* The car keys were in the jacket."

"We can call my dad," Marilyn said. "He's pretty laid back about stuff like this. Says always call him if I'm stuck. He'd rather have me call than get into more trouble if I didn't."

"Okay, Marilyn's dad to the rescue." Jane gave her a tight smile.

"What's that up ahead? Is that what you guys saw back there?" Rob pointed at some turbulence in the water near the center archway under the bridge. The waves were disturbed and going in all directions, spraying water up in the air that reflected off the lights from the bridge.

"That's a lot of splashing. Looks just like our wake did. When the boat came under the bridge, it reflected the light." Jane started beating her palm against the back of George's seat. "What do we do? Can we go around it? Or through it?"

George shook his head. "No way I'm driving into the middle of that if we don't know what it is. The water is a little shallower on the sides of the bridge, but we're a motorboat. We don't have much draw except for the ladder in the back. I'm going right." And he veered the boat toward the archway on the Buffalo side.

They drew parallel with the disturbed section of water, and Jane started to breathe a sigh of relief when the turbulence suddenly stopped. A minute later, the water erupted again ahead of them on the shore side, causing a huge wave to wash up against the stone piling that supported the bridge's center and right-hand arches.

Moments later, they felt and heard a big bump against the boat. It threw Jane to the side, and she would have fallen but for Rob's tight grip on her arm. She let out a shriek.

"Well, that's not good. Let's get the hell out of here." George gunned the engine as they passed under the archway. The boat started going so fast that the bow lifted a bit out of the water going downriver.

"Okay, everybody keep an eye out. Rob, you look to the left. Marilyn, you look to the right, and Jane, can you see behind us? I don't want it to sneak up on us… if there *is* an 'it.'"

They all nodded in agreement. Jane carefully turned around, holding onto both seats, and watched the deepening wake spewing out behind them. "Okay, I don't see anything. You guys?"

"Just holler if you do," George said. "And hold on, for Christ's sake."

The rest of the return trip passed uneventfully as they left the brighter lights of the bridge and downtown area. Nothing snuck up on them in the water, and no further sightings of unexplained turbulence crossed their route.

As they approached the marina, George turned off the eight-track player but left the running lights on. "Last thing I want to do now is cruise around in the dark. Think we've had enough fun for one night, don't you, guys?"

They all nodded quietly. Once the boat was safely docked, everyone grabbed their stuff and tossed the empty beer cans in the garbage on their way up the ramp. The marina was deserted and dark as it was after midnight. The light from a nearby Utica Club billboard shone down on the four teens in the parking lot as they headed for the payphone by the marina office. *No artificial bubbles! We age beer the natural way.*

George swore under his breath. "Goddammit, all my change went overboard in the jacket. I don't have a dime."

Marilyn pulled a change purse out of her macramé bag and moved to the payphone. "My mom insists I keep an emergency stash. When I was younger, I'd always have a dime in each of my penny loafers."

"Are you kidding?" Rob gaped at her. "I just thought girls were being, I don't know, cute or something when they did that."

Jane hushed him while Marilyn dropped a dime in the slot, waited for dial tone, then spun the rotary. They all held their breath until she gave a thumbs-up sign.

"Dad? You know how you always say to call if I need help? Well, we kinda have a problem here..."

"Thanks, Mr. Collins. We appreciate the ride." Rob's shoulders slumped as they slid out of the car in front of their little Tudor house in Eggertsville. He and Jane waved to their friends as the car pulled off, and Rob smiled when Marilyn flashed him a peace sign in return.

Their father's '68 Mustang sat in the driveway, the moonlight glinting off the green metallic paint and gold racing stripes. Turning to Jane, Rob said, "Well, let's hope Dad doesn't wake up and notice we were out. At least I don't have to work tomorrow."

"Yeah." She patted him lightly on the shoulder, whispering as they headed around to the back door. "Okay, gotta be quiet inside. Let's talk in the morning."

The twins snuck in and headed to their bedrooms. Jane lay awake for a long time.

Chapter Three

1969: Saturday, June 7

In the morning, the twins wound up sleeping late. Their father had left a note on the chalkboard hanging in the kitchen next to the wall phone, saying that he'd been called into work since the project at the dam was getting busy.

The two siblings sat at the oak kitchen table, slumped on chairs with woven cane backs and vinyl seat cushions in bright yellow that matched the Formica counters. The yellow gingham place mats coordinated with the faded cafe curtains on the window over the sink.

"Good thing it's a Saturday," Jane said, yawning as she poured Rice Krispies into a bowl. "I don't know if this counts as breakfast or lunch. Pass the milk, okay?"

Rob pushed the glass quart bottle toward her. "So, what do you think? Was it all a dream?"

"I don't know, but I want to see what was out there by the bridge."

His eyes widened. "You mean… go out on the boat again? Are you crazy?"

"Yeah, I guess we pretty much know that I'm the crazy one here." She snorted. "But if there's evidence that would show we weren't dreaming the whole thing, then I want to know what it is. And besides, it's taken us ten years to go back out on the water, and I don't want to be afraid of it anymore."

He stared at her for a moment, then walked to the yellow wall phone and dialed. "George. Hey, man. Everything cool with your parents about the keys?" He nodded.

"Good. Hey, uh… Jane wants to go out again and see the bridge. You game?" He held the phone away from his ear. "Yeah, yeah, I know she's crazy. But will you take us?"

Jane snorted. "I heard that!"

Rob hung the receiver back on the wall. "He says if we ride our bikes there, he can meet us at the marina. He's gotta go anyway to pick up the car. His dad had an extra key."

"Now? On our bikes? That's like, what, seven miles?" She took a deep breath. "Okay, let me get dressed. Holy cow, I can't believe we're doing this."

She shoveled the rest of her cereal into her mouth then ran to grab her Polaroid as Rob wrote a note to their dad on the chalkboard telling him where they were going.

Leaving the bikes parked under a tree, the three headed upriver in the bright spring afternoon sunshine—along with Marilyn, who had hitched a ride to the marina and met them there. Jane had chuckled to herself while getting dressed when she'd heard Rob calling her.

Marilyn wore a pair of short shorts and a striped top. She craned her neck to see all around. "Looks different in the daytime. I mean, look at all the sunshine and all the other boats. Lots more traffic."

Jane grinned and leaned forward. "Yeah, well, it is a lovely day on the weekend. Everybody else is out for fun now that they're off work. We, on the other hand, are on a mission."

"And to help fuel our mission, I brought some pop!" Marilyn pulled some cans of Mountain Dew out of the bag she'd been carrying, then passed them around.

"All right!" Rob toasted them all with his can. "To my crazy sister, Jane."

"I'll drink to that!" George answered with a tipsy lisp, and they all giggled at Dick Martin's well-worn line from *Laugh-In*.

It took almost an hour for them to get up to the Peace Bridge because of the extra water traffic. Jane sat in the same spot on the bench as the previous night, trailing her hand through the spray. She had her camera tucked between her feet so it wouldn't get wet.

George kept an eye on the other boats around them. "Well, we're getting close to the bridge. Where do we want to look first?"

"How about if we go through the middle to the other side like we did last night?" Jane suggested. "We should check out the bridge first. There was that big wave at the end."

Rob nodded. "Yeah, cool. And if we don't see anything, we can go farther out on Lake Erie."

The boat approached the bridge, with others both behind and to either side of them. Jane withdrew her hand from the water and stared out the right side. Marilyn and Rob looked to the left at the other pillar forming the center arch. As they passed underneath, they craned their necks around, scanning the abutments until they were on the lake side of the bridge.

George moved out of the main traffic pattern, throttling down to pause for a moment. The four took a minute to scan the lake.

"Okay, anybody see anything to investigate? Nope? Okay, let's go back through on the right, like we did last night." He turned the boat and headed toward the bridge, going more slowly this time as there was less traffic on the side arch. They all looked out the left side of the boat at where the turbulence had erupted the night before.

"You cats see that blob up there? Holy cow. What the heck is that?" Marilyn pointed at a dark shape that rested atop the base of the bridge pillar.

George steered a bit closer and slowed. "I think maybe we can reach it with the boat hook if somebody stands on the cabin roof. Jane, Rob?"

He looked between the two twins, who each stared at him with big eyes, then patted Marilyn on the shoulder. "I think you're elected, California girl."

Marilyn paled and shook her head. "Oh, *hell* no. You want *me* to go up on top of the boat and get that… that *thing*?"

"C'mon, I've gotta drive the boat, and you've got better sea legs than these two. Grab the boat hook on top of the roof." He pointed overhead. "I'll circle around again."

She took a deep breath. "Okay, sock it to me!" Marilyn stood and pried the long collapsible aluminum pole from its holder on the roof. She followed George's directions and extended the hook by twisting the end, making the pole even longer, then crawled up onto the cabin's roof and crouched there, holding on.

George looped in a slow circle around the pillar — carefully avoiding the oncoming boats. The next time around, he went as close to the stone as he dared and put the boat in neutral, telling Rob to keep an eye out for boats behind them. "And Jane, keep an eye on the water for your fishy friend."

She barked a laugh and gave a wry grin. "Friend, indeed." She scanned the water around them, then turned and snapped a picture of Marilyn with her Polaroid, grabbing the square of film as it came out of the bottom of the camera. "Let's document what we're doing here."

Marilyn poked at the dark blob sticking out from the ridge on top of the post. "Think I've snagged something!" A quick yank and an oblong, three-foot-long mass of seaweed landed on the floor of the open cabin with a heavy thud.

Rob pinched his nose shut. "Damn, that stinks! What... what is it? That was too heavy for just seaweed." He started to nudge it with his toe.

"Hey, wait a sec!" Jane cried, and Rob jumped back.

"What? What's it gonna do?"

She took a picture of the blob, still fanning the first Polaroid print in her hand as it developed. "I want to keep a record of what we find here. Wish I'd had this last night."

When she was done, Rob squatted down and pulled the mass of seaweed apart while he tried not to breathe through his nose. "There's something wrapped up in the middle here." He unwound the last layer and revealed the front half of a huge fish carcass.

George glanced over his shoulder while keeping the boat steady. "Oh, damn, I've never seen one that big. It's a giant sturgeon. They've been pretty rare since my dad was a kid. My grandfather caught some sturgeon in Lake Erie and the Niagara River during the fifties, and he still brags about being in the newspaper."

"Huh. A sturgeon. Is that what we saw?" Rob tilted his head as he stared at the stinking mess. "It's big but doesn't seem big enough."

"Guys, stand back. There's something else up here," Marilyn called down from where she'd been watching atop the cabin. She turned and poked into the crevice again, pulling out another wet shape that plopped at her feet on the roof. "Oh, you're not gonna believe this. Yo, this thing stinks."

Marilyn held half of George's denim jacket up and away from her, between thumb and forefinger. She turned her face to the side while checking the pockets. "No keys. Sorry, man. Nothing helpful, although it's weird that wave washed the jacket up here. Guess we may as well go back now?"

Rob reached up and helped her down from the roof, sneaking a kiss as she moved past. Her feet just touched the cabin floor when a scream from the main part of the river made them all jump. Marilyn clutched Rob's arms to keep her balance.

"Now what?" Jane ran to the gunwale and scanned the nearby boats. "Anybody see anything? Wait, look! He's going under!" She pointed to an old motorboat that had collided with the bridge abutment and dumped one of the occupants overboard. A teen boy was leaning over a gash in the edge of the motorboat, trying to reach someone in the water who kept slipping under the surface.

"Hold on! Man overboard! Jane, keep pointing at the guy in the water so we don't lose him." George turned their boat toward the collision scene. "Marilyn, you've got the boat hook. Get ready to try and reach the guy!"

Rob steadied Marilyn by holding her hips as they neared the collision site. The teen in the motorboat sat back and waved them to come closer. George slowed the boat, and Marilyn leaned over the edge, extending the aluminum pole out to the guy in the water.

"Grab on! We'll pull you in!" Jane's voice came out shrill with nerves. She focused on the scene, still pointing at him with one hand, and waved the other in the air with excitement. "You'll be okay!"

The guy reached out for the boat hook. His fingers almost touched it when suddenly a huge shape came in from the bow. It burst out of the water, knocked the boat hook out of Marilyn's hand, and pushed the man underwater!

The sleek, muscular shape passed between the two boats. A long fin rippled along its gray back, throwing spray on the teens in George's boat. Jane's mouth dropped. The creature locked its blue eye with hers as it went by, sending a shock of connection that rocked her on her heels. She felt frozen as the moment stretched out—it seemed to hang in midair forever until it submerged with a splash. The final whip of its tail sent their boat sideways away from the guy in the water.

"Ohmygod, ohmygod!" She continued pointing at where the man submerged. "What the hell was that? Wait, where's the guy?" His head popped up from under the waves, and he sputtered and flailed. Jane pointed again, guiding George back to meet him. Marilyn picked herself up from where she'd been knocked down and ran to the ladder on the back of the boat. She climbed halfway into the water and linked arms with the guy, then Rob helped drag him up.

Once he was safely aboard, they pulled alongside the other craft which was damaged but still afloat. The teen onboard was shaking but insisted his friend transfer to his boat. "Really, man, it was all my fault. We were sort of racing the wind, which I guess was dumb so close to the bridge. Some sort of uh, I guess, a big wave came up and made me swerve. I guess it splashed off the abutment. But why did you drop your pole? You almost had him!" He looked at Marilyn with an eyebrow raised.

"You didn't see anything… weird?" Jane asked. She scanned the surrounding water with half her attention. "Huh, I see that there's damage on *both* sides of your boat, so it can't just be from hitting the bridge on one side."

The teen shrugged and ran his fingers along the gash torn in the gunwale. "Ha-ha, I thought a giant eel jumped out and splashed you, but we just shared a coupla Alice B. Toklas brownies, if ya know what I mean, so… I'm not sure if I really saw anything or not. But it still floats, so we're cool. We're cool, man."

Once they helped the soaking wet guy back to the other boat, the four gathered around the driver's seat. "That guy was high as a kite! Shouldn't be out on the water like that." George shook his head.

Marilyn snorted. "Says the guy who was chugging beer out here last night!"

He held his hands up in surrender. "Okay, point taken. But it sounds like something made them run into the bridge. And… I was busy driving, but you guys didn't see anything leap out of the water, right? It's just the hippie being crazy?"

Rob and Jane exchanged glances and then shrugged. They all nodded.

Together they trolled in circles a few more times around the bridge and the area where they had been the night before, with no further results. Eventually, they called it quits and headed back to the marina. On the way back, Marilyn and Jane firmed up their plans to see Niagara Falls the next day.

Once they had docked, Rob turned to the others. "Well, thanks for helping us look, guys. Can we pay you to gas the boat, George?" When he shook his head, Rob went on. "Our dad's probably working late. How about dinner on us at Carroll's, then?"

"Carol? Is that a friend of yours?" Marilyn pouted at Rob. "You never mentioned her before."

George grinned. "Nope! Carroll's is the best fast food in the area. I'll never turn down a burger with pickles."

Chapter Four

After a quick dinner at the local fast-food joint, Jane and Rob unloaded their bikes from the trunk of George's car and waved as he drove off. Their father, Edward, met them at the back door after they put their bikes in the garage and eyed their still-damp shoes.

He sniffed and wrinkled his nose. "I didn't think it was raining anywhere, kids. How'd you get all wet?"

The twins looked at each other and shrugged. "You tell him," Rob said.

Jane took a deep breath. "Dad, there's something we want to talk to you about. We went out on George's boat with him, and some… weird stuff happened."

Their father's eyebrows went way up. "Okay, then. Come on in and dry off, and then let's sit down. I'll put on some water for tea."

Jane hadn't noticed she was shivering — the idea of a hot cup of tea sounded like just what she wanted. "Cool, Dad, we'll be down in just a few."

A few minutes later, she cradled a mug of Red Rose tea in one hand, enjoying both the warmth and the reassuring feel of it. She nibbled on a cookie; Rob had already finished three. For once, everyone ignored the dinnertime news show playing on the little black-and-white television on the counter.

"So. What's all this about?" Edward looked back and forth between his children. "Last I knew, you guys were afraid of going out on the water. You went out on the boat with George?"

Rob nodded. "Yeah, he's been trying to get us to go out for years, but… well, you know."

Their father nodded, and the crease between his eyebrows deepened. "I wish I could have helped you guys get used to the water much sooner, after your mom… after the accident."

Jane put her hand over his. "Dad, we know it's hard for you, too. But we finally did it. We finally went out on the boat last night."

His head jerked up. "Last night? So why are you wet now?"

Jane took a deep breath and started to tell him all that had happened. She was nearly done when the local news broadcast an announcement that stopped her words mid-sentence: "Local man attacked by a sea monster in the Niagara River."

They all turned to the set. The news reporter was kneeling at a marina dock, next to the boat they had come across that day. The camera zoomed in on the gash taken out of the boat's edge. "The owner of the boat and his guest report that they were attacked by a huge creature in the Niagara River, right under the Peace Bridge. It nearly sank their boat and tried to eat the one who fell in the water. The man was saved by four good Samaritans in another boat who chased the creature away."

The teen they had helped could be heard in the background. "It was a monster, I tell you!"

When the news report was over, their father sat quietly, head down and seemingly deep in thought. Finally, he looked up at the two of them and gave a nod. "All right. There's a lot that I have to tell you about the family. And what actually happened to your mom."

Rob and Jane looked at each other and leaned in across the table.

"You know that your mom's family has been in this area for generations." Edward sat back and steepled his fingers together. "Grandma and Grandpa lived on the south shore of Lake Erie, and I'm sure you've heard me say that they ran a carnival. Well, it wasn't a stable source of income for them, especially in the early days. Seasonal crowds, people had limited money at the end of the Depression, you get the picture. But Grandma's side of the family had a special ability that had to do with the water. However, it took two of them to make it work."

Rob put down his half-eaten cookie. "It had to do with the water? Were they fishermen way back then?"

"I'm not sure about that part, although fish *is* sort of the answer." Dad took a deep breath and dropped his face into his hands.

"Dad! Are you okay?" Jane jumped up and hugged him.

Rob joined her and rubbed his father's back. "C'mon, Dad, you can tell us. Please."

Their father's shoulders shook, then he took a deep breath and patted their arms. "I'm okay. I'm okay, thank you, kids."

"I can tell this is really hard for you to talk about, Dad." Jane kept a hand on his arm as she and Rob sat back down.

"Yeah, but it's way past time you guys learned more about the family. Maybe the best thing is to give you Grandma's diary to read. I know you've seen some of the pictures in the old photo albums, but I never showed you the diary before. Do you want to see it?"

Both twins bobbed their heads—Jane more vigorously than Rob. Edward led them into the living room and unlocked a drawer in the big rolltop desk in the corner. He drew out a leather-bound book with a faded pink ribbon tied around it.

"There are some amazing memories in here, all about when Grandma Emily and Grandpa Douglas were married, and when your mother Rachel was a toddler." He looked down at the journal. "Rachel had grown up reading it, and your grandma gave it to her when we got married. I remember your mother sitting and reading this when you guys were little. She loved her mother's story." He looked up at the two of them with a soft smile.

"It was a long time before Rachel let me read it. She said she wasn't sure I could understand, but that she had married me because she hoped I could." Tears glistened in his eyes. "I've tried to live up to what she expected of me, raising the two of you without her. I wish she were here to tell me what to do, but I've waited until I thought you could understand."

"Dad. C'mon, it's okay," Rob said. "We're pretty much grown up now."

Edward smiled at his son. "Of course, you are, and you're both good people. I just have to warn you that this is not an easy read. It may be scary or upsetting, but I'm here to talk about it when you're done." He patted the cover of the diary, then passed it to Jane.

"Here you go. All I ask is that the book doesn't leave the house. It was very precious to your mother."

Jane slowly reached out and took the volume from him.

"We'll take good care of it, Dad. Thank you." She turned and looked at Rob. "Do you want to read it together, or take turns?"

"Why don't you read it, Sis, and you can fill me in." He gave her a lopsided grin. "Anyway, we know you're the smarty-pants reader in the family."

She grinned, taking a bit of comfort from their usual jokes, and hugged the book to her chest. "C'mon, you big doofus. Even though you play sports, you're pretty darn smart too, you know."

"Okay, kids. Thank you for being encouraging." Edward rubbed his face with his hand for a moment. "You were so little. I was never sure how to start this conversation with you, or when you would be ready. But since it looks like you guys took things into your own hands, it's clearly time for you to dive in. So to speak."

Rob snickered. "Good one, Dad."

"Let's go watch the Smothers Brothers, Rob. I think it's coming on now." Edward headed toward the kitchen, calling back to her over his shoulder. "The relevant part of the story starts in the spring of 1939. Holler if you have any questions, kiddo, okay?"

Jane nodded and waved a hand vaguely in their direction as they left, already curling up in her favorite reading chair in the corner. "You got it, Dad. Thanks."

She untied the pink ribbon and opened her grandmother's diary. A sprig of pressed, dried flowers fell into her lap. She traced the outline of the tiny, faded blue flowers with one finger and then sniffed them, but no aroma remained.

"I know these. We have them growing out in the backyard. Forget-me-nots." She carefully placed the dried flowers on the side table and started reading Grandma Emily's words.

It started with the family's earlier years when her grandparents were married and her mother Rachel was born, during what Jane gathered was the Great Depression, although they didn't seem to call it that while they were living it. Jane hadn't thought about how hard things were for the family back then.

She was fascinated by the stories of how they set up the carnival—apparently as an act of desperation since they could not get regular jobs—and tried to survive the first few seasons. After several hours of reading, she got to the part her father had mentioned in the spring of 1939.

CHAPTER FIVE

FRIDAY, APRIL 21, 1939

Well, Dear Diary, we are still waiting for more snow to melt so we can start up the carnival again. Douglas got the rest of the trees cleared off the lot last fall to make the midway bigger so we can sell more food, but then the snows came, so we haven't been able to do any work. The dirt road coming in off the main road from town has a bunch of ruts in it after the harsh winter, so I hope it's good enough. But we'll finally have plenty of parking once they do get here.

Rachel and I spent some time working on her letters over the winter. It made me so proud when my little four-year-old recited all of her ABCs to her father at breakfast this morning! Amazing to think we might have another baby on the way, but I'm not sure when to tell Douglas. He has so much on his mind right now.

Can you believe the blue forget-me-nots survived the winter? Douglas gave me the seeds last year because he knew I loved them from when I was a girl in Scotland, and I just sprinkled the seeds outside the barn door. First, I was amazed that they even grew in that rocky part, but they were tenacious. Now they're peeking out between the patches of snow and blooming the most beautiful shade of bright blue. I told him they match his eyes.

I had Douglas tell the men to roll out the main tent from the barn, and then they moved my sewing machine in there for me to make patches. Poor tent is so old, but we can't afford a new one. I have to say it was a tight fit with all the benches in there.

We got a good report on a couple of the new entertainment acts, too. One guy is an axe-thrower and says his brother can work security; another one apparently specializes in doing tricks with a whip. So, there's that. They should be arriving in mid-May, but I just don't know if we'll have enough entertainment to draw the crowds this year. Time will tell, Dear Diary. Good night.

SUNDAY, MAY 14, 1939

Dear Diary, I'm sorry I've been so busy and haven't written here in a while. There is so much to do for the carnival! It's all very exciting. We'll be setting up the tent soon. Almost done patching it.

Several more acts for the main stage look quite exciting. A young woman in a pink tutu can apparently do ballet on the back of a horse. I never even knew you could do that! She seems quite good, although the horse eats a lot. As do the dogs in the performing dog act.

We're doing a soft opening this weekend to be ready for season kickoff and then Memorial Day on the 30th. That's when I think more people will start coming to the carnival. We're going to have a big show with some fireworks and flags to kick it off. Must run, Dear Diary.

1969: SATURDAY, JUNE 7

Jane looked up and realized that either her brother or her dad had brought her a fresh cup of tea while she was reading. She'd been so absorbed that she hadn't noticed. She sipped the cooling tea and thought about how her mother might have felt, reading about herself as a small child.

It made Jane happy to know that her mother had been a bright little kid, too, and she had a hazy memory of learning letters from her. Maybe that was where she got her love of reading — a family tradition?

She'd read enough of her grandmother's diary that she better understood the economic peril that her grandparents had been in and marveled that they had been resourceful enough to run a carnival at the end of the Depression. But what was the scary part her father had mentioned?

What she read didn't seem like a diary anymore, but more like she was reading a good book and couldn't wait to find out what happened next.

Jane took the tea up to her room and got into her nightgown. She curled up in bed, opened the diary again, and dove into Grandma Emily's story as if she were living it.

Chapter Six

"Douglas?" Where had he gotten to? I needed some help with moving the tent to patch the next section.

He came in from the side door of the barn, crossing to where I was, slipped his arms around me from behind, and kissed my neck, moving my long red braid to the other side. "How are you holding up, sweetie?"

I leaned back into the embrace. "Not bad, handsome. But my eyes sure are tired. Kinda hard to light up the barn well enough to see without burning it down." I rubbed my eyes, suddenly conscious of how much they ached once I said the words. "Can you get some of the roustabouts to help move the tent? I have a patch ready, but I need to get under the canvas."

He nodded and stepped to the door. "Nathan! Jake! Come give us a hand, boys." He waved and grinned out the door.

In a minute, two strapping farmhands showed up, and together the three of them maneuvered a corner of the giant circus tent to a different spot over the old wagon in the center of the space, following my directions.

"Thank you, boys. Now I can get to it." I dragged the patch over to the spot where I had been working, brought over my needle and leather palm protector, and got to work sewing it on. "Only ten more miles of seams to go."

Late that night, Douglas made me stop work and come see what they had set up so far on the midway. I tied off the patch where I had been working and checked on Rachel, who was asleep on her little mattress on the floor of our room out back, sucking her thumb and hugging her rag doll. Tiptoeing out, I closed the door quietly and grabbed my coat from the peg.

We walked through the area where the main tent would soon be set up—we were hopeful the snow was done for the spring—and over to the midway road. We still stepped over and around big puddles in the dirt road, and I made a note in my head that we'd need to add a new layer of gravel to keep it passable on rainy days.

The booths along the midway were mostly repaired from the winter, and I grinned at the empty skeleton of the various stalls. On the right, we passed games of chance. The floating rubber ducks were always my favorite—pick a number and place a wager that yours would be selected, and the carnie plucked a duck out of the water to reveal the winning number on the bottom.

Next was the booth where people threw darts at balloons for a chance to win a prize. My mind filled the shelf across the back wall with stuffed animals, and my hand slipped absently to my belly. Plenty of time to tell Douglas about my suspicions, and I wanted to be sure. If he knew we were having another baby, he'd worry about me working too hard, and this was the busy time to get the carnival set up, or else we'd be bankrupt by the Fourth of July.

He put his arm around my shoulders, and I leaned into him. He kissed the top of my head. "What do you think, sweetie? Coming along?"

"You bet, mister. I can already see the crowds of people here, enjoying cotton candy and funnel cakes." I grinned. "And spending lots of money on the rides!"

When we got to the end of the midway, we turned back to our room in the barn. After all, why spend money for a house when there was a perfectly good barn to sleep in? I chuckled. Of course, it was just a one-room shed attached to the back of the barn.

Mentally, I shook my head—if my grandmother in Scotland could see me, she'd wonder why on earth my mother had brought us here. Of course, there was a reason they'd had to leave, but the family didn't talk about the secret much. At all. And certainly not with outsiders.

I braced myself for another chilly night as we got ready for bed, putting on multiple layers of wool sweaters I had inherited when my mother passed ten years before. And wished she and my father had met Douglas before their accident.

FRIDAY, MAY 26, 1939

The Friday before Memorial Day dawned bright and clear, and we'd been busy since the moment we opened our eyes. There was a lot of running around, and some things were not where they were supposed to be, but all in all, opening day had been going well. A small but steady stream of people came in from the parking lot in the evening after their workday was done.

Most of the ladies dressed stylishly, even though we were still coming out of the rough times and money was tight. I took note because we women felt the pressure to look beautiful on a dime, and they had dressed up for an evening out! They all wore a lot more makeup than I did — unless I was going to be in the ring, like tonight.

I saw many linen-like rayon dresses with tiny flowers, with pleats on the front and a double collar, some made of dotted swiss fabrics. Many fit slim through the hips but loose through the body and fell to mid-calf. They either buttoned up the front or used those newer zippers that were all the rage because they actually cost less than buttons! The variety of hats on the ladies was astounding. Some were from the previous decade, judging by the style, but the ladies all looked lovely.

The men's suits sported big shoulders and then nipped in at the waist. Some were clearly old, but just about every man was all spiffed up and wore their hair slicked back under a nice fedora hat.

The smell of hotdogs, sausage with onions and peppers, and fried potatoes filled the air. It made me a bit queasy but also signaled the beginning of the carnival season, so my heart rejoiced — when I had time to think about it — or else it was just nerves. This year, I had a part in the evening show under the tent.

To be honest, part of me was still worried about whether my patches would hold! It had taken all available hands to raise the tent, and I glanced nervously up at the seams on the roof overhead. Douglas caught my look and grinned. He pulled me to him for a kiss with one hand around the back of my head, but I resisted more than a light peck even though he looked so handsome in his black tails and top hat.

"Careful! My makeup!"

He grinned and chucked my chin with one knuckle. "Love you, sweetie. We're gonna knock 'em dead! Right, Rachel?"

Our little one looked up as he rubbed the top of her head. She was playing with her rag doll on the floor behind the curtain where I had folded a quilt for her. "Right, Daddie!"

He peeked out at the crowd seated on the benches, and I could see his gaze moving from person to person, mentally counting heads. It looked like enough people for a profitable evening. I crossed my fingers and hoped it would keep on like that all weekend—and through the summer.

The music started up, played by an old stumblebum on the ancient piano in the corner; then the young guy on a washboard drum started a drill of notes that built faster and louder until Douglas stepped out from the opening in the tent where we'd been waiting.

"Ladies and gentlemen! Welcome to our premier show of the season! You are clearly the cleverest folks in the area to get here early and see all the great offerings before your friends do. Go tell them all how much fun you've had tonight! Come back again and bring them with you. We have a show every Friday and Saturday night, and a special one this Tuesday for Memorial Day!"

The crowd burst into applause, and Douglas bowed.

"Thank you, thank you! Now, first up, for those of you who love something exciting: Abe and the axe! He will amaze you with his precision, accuracy, and strength! I present to you, Abe the Amazing Axe-man!"

He bowed again, gesturing to the other entrance with a flourish as a handsome young man with a full mustache stepped out, wearing pants and suspenders over a white long-sleeve shirt. Abe flourished a huge, long-handled axe as he turned to face the crowd in each direction, then started flipping it up in the air and catching it, over and over. He stopped after a moment, regarded the axe, and then looked at the crowd.

"I know what you're thinking. 'That axe isn't sharp. I could do that.' *AM I RIGHT?*" Some of the crowd laughed and jeered.

He beckoned to me, and I pushed a little cart across the open area of the ring. Abe grabbed one of the logs from the cart, threw it up in the air, and swung at it like a baseball—striking the log and embedding the blade so far that the log stuck on the axe. He lifted it over his head with one hand, beckoning to the crowd for applause with the other. I strutted away to the side and got a hug from Douglas when I stepped out of the ring.

When the cheering started to die down, he made a big show of prying the log off the blade, then lifted two more long axes off the cart. Abe stopped and visibly centered himself, then tossed the axes into the air one after the other, catching them by the handles as they came down and juggling them in a continuous flow. Every time one came down, it looked like he would miss it and it would cleave his skull, but he effortlessly stuck out a hand at the last minute and snatched it out of the air, tossing it up again a fraction of a second later until his hands moved in a continuous blur.

The crowd roared. Several people in the stands turned toward a woman who appeared to have swooned.

Douglas and I gripped each other's hands so tightly that I couldn't feel my fingers, and when Abe caught the last axe and went for a deep bow, I clapped so hard that my hand woke up in a hurry!

The rest of the night passed in almost a blur. The crowd got more enthusiastic with each act, and from time to time, I also looked out the tent opening to peek at the midway since my little piece in the show was not until the end. The carnival grounds weren't packed, just like the tent still had plenty of open seats, but people moved from stall to stall, and folks stood in line at the various food booths. Everyone seemed to be having a good time.

Late that night, after all the people were gone and the lights were all out, Douglas and I sat together in our little room reviewing the receipts while Rachel slept on her pallet on the floor. As tired as he was, he had even made the effort to bring me a little bouquet of my favorite flowers from outside the back door. I admired the forget-me-nots in the mug of water on the table.

I counted the money, mostly coins, and he checked over the list of ticket sales from the man at the entry gate. He finished first and sat watching me, smiling despite the tired lines on his face. When I finished, he pushed his tally sheet over toward me with a pencil.

"So? How'd we do?" He eyed the pile of cash.

I held up one finger as I wrote the totals for each denomination of coins and the few bills on his sheet at the bottom, checking my notes so as not to rely on my memory. I was too tired to keep numbers in my head the way I normally would on a regular day. I circled the number.

We both leaned in and bumped heads over the paper. Sitting back, he rubbed his forehead, and we both laughed—in part because of the collision and in part because our tallies nearly matched, at least close enough. There were always discrepancies with people taking money and making change, and it would have been very odd to have the numbers match exactly. But it was well within our margin of error and more than we thought we'd take in on the opening night.

Maybe we'd be able to support ourselves, after all.

We swept the coins into cloth bags for each denomination. Douglas placed the cash in the lockbox, then stowed it under our bed — once he looked around to be sure nobody was peering through the windows. It surely wouldn't do to be robbed on our first night!

Chapter Seven

The next few weeks passed in a blur. We were either putting on a show, cleaning up after the crowds had left for the evening, or getting ready for the next day. Douglas and I were very pleased to pay all the entertainers, midway carnies, and cooks their full salary each week! After so many years of being impoverished, all our people appreciated having real money in their hands.

We rode into town and arranged with the butcher for more hotdogs and chipped beef to be delivered for the food stands. I smiled to myself because the butcher's wife was quite smitten with Abe, the axe-thrower. It just showed that we had made the correct decision by moving his act to be the finale!

Douglas stopped in at the local tavern to spread the word about the show. "Never hurts to mingle with the townies now and then, right?"

I raised my eyebrows, as experience had shown it was never good to mix with townies. Plus, it wasn't proper for me and Rachel to go in there with him, so we went to the grocer and arranged our order. I splurged and got her a lollipop. We didn't have to wait too long at the truck for Douglas; she had her sucker to keep her busy. We leaned against the tailgate, with her sitting on the bumper, watching the passersby. A pair of men walked past wearing work boots and heavy cotton wide-leg pants with suspenders, but they had a hungry look to them that made me think maybe they didn't have jobs.

On the way home, Douglas told me about visiting the tavern. "Well, sweetie, there was a good number of folks in there for an afternoon, but that's nothing new these days even though the newspaper keeps saying the recession is over. A lot of them said they didn't have a job, but their wives did. But at least that gave them enough money to go out with their friends and even come to the show."

He broke into a huge grin and squeezed my knee closest to him. "The show! A coupla men recognized me, and one even bought me a drink. They liked the show!"

I leaned over and rested my head on his shoulder as he drove, with Rachel on my right knee. "It's great that they liked it! And that means you saved your drink money, so we girls get an ice cream soda or milkshake next time we come to town."

"I was thinking the same thing." He chuckled, then sobered. "And Abe was in there too. Seemed like he has quite the following."

I nodded. It seemed like Abe had that effect on a lot of people.

Chapter Eight

Friday, June 16, 1939

Douglas and I sat counting the money as usual after the night's packed show. We went through the ticket receipts, the money from the food stalls, and the house take from all the games of chance on the midway. When we were done, we sat back at our little table and stared at each other. Douglas pressed his palms together in front of his face and tapped on his forehead, looking down.

I pulled the tally sheet back in front of me, then pulled out our ledger book and compared the numbers from the shows on the first opening weekend and on Memorial Day when we'd only had partial crowds. I began to rub the fingers of one hand with the other in worry.

"It's not just me, right? Douglas?" I put out a hand and touched his arm. "The numbers here say we took in less money than we did at our opening show. But all the seats were full in the tent, and the midway was packed. We even ran out of food at the sausage stand. So…?"

He sat back, shoulders slumped. "Yes. We should have a lot more money than we do. So, why are we short? Let's count it again."

"Honey, we've counted it three times. The money isn't there. It doesn't make sense. It's not like there's just someone shortchanging us on the ticket take, but *everything* is lower than it should be. I *know* we calculated how much the food cost us and how much money we'd take in from selling it all, but we're short."

I glanced over my shoulder to make sure that Rachel was still asleep. She wouldn't understand our words, but my clever girl would know that we were upset. Golly, we were more than upset.

"All right, we still need to go into town this week and order more food for the next two weekends. But it's going to be tight." He rubbed his face with his hands.

I nodded. "The girl and I can skip the milkshake. And we should keep an eye on everyone around here to see if it looks like anything shady is going on."

He barked a laugh. I held a finger to my lips, and he lowered his voice.

"Isn't that rich? The owners of a carnival looking out for shady business."

We stowed the money in the cash box under the bed and crawled under the covers for a restless night of sleep.

Little Rachel and I spent the whole next day walking up and down the midway and the food stalls; she enjoyed the hustle and bustle while I looked for signs that someone was shorting us out on their take. The customers — even though I was now a carnie, I hated to call them rubes, like some of the others did — were lined up for games of chance. They were usually males, often accompanied by a female for whom they were showing off and trying to win a prize.

I paused near the kewpie doll game, watching from the side of the stall so Carl wouldn't see us as he ran his game.

He called out to the next customer in line, a teenage boy with a girl next to him, each of them dressed up and self-conscious of the other. "Here ya go, son. You look like an athlete! Just knock down three kewpie dolls, is all. Think you can do it? There's a prize for the little lady if you do!"

The girl blushed. The teenage boy paid him some coins, then got a small ball in exchange. To win, he had five chances to knock over three of the little kewpie dolls lined up on the shelf at the back of the stall. The little celluloid figures had big eyes in adorable baby faces and stood with their arms outstretched to the sides.

It seemed like it would be easy, but I knew that the games were set up to not be in favor of the customer. Some of the kewpie dolls were weighted on the bottom so that they had to be hit low down or they wouldn't tip. And the ball itself was not a typical rubber ball — it was also weighted inside but often asymmetrically so that it wouldn't throw as expected. But most customers were so caught up in the excitement of the carnival and in showing off for a young lady that they didn't notice.

The teenager flipped the ball up in the air and caught it with a flick of his wrist. My heart sank. He looked like a baseball player.

Ringer. He took a stance, hurled the ball at one of the kewpie dolls—and missed.

"Bad luck, young man, but you look like you've got an arm on you. Four more chances to make the little lady proud." The gamekeeper returned the ball. "Lou Gehrig's been slipping the last coupla seasons. Maybe you can take his place!"

The youth ducked his head at that, then took his second shot and hit one of the kewpie dolls—but the ball bounced off. A group of young onlookers laughed good-naturedly, but the boy's ears got red as Carl gave him the ball. He tossed it in the air a few more times, watching as it left his hand and returned. His next two throws were so hard that he knocked down two dolls, leaving him one more chance to knock down the third kewpie.

I watched Carl reach down under the counter as he retrieved the ball for the last round, and from my angle could clearly see him swap out the ball for a different one. The boy's final throw went wild, confirming my suspicion that the last ball was differently weighted. When the gang of younger boys laughed and jeered, the teenager demanded to see the ball, and Carl expertly switched them again before handing it back.

"What's the problem, young man? You did great! Hardly anyone gets two down. Well done! You wanna play again? I bet you can win!"

The youth felt in his pockets, but his hands came back empty. He shrugged and shook his head, then turned and stalked away with the girl hurrying to catch up.

"It's okay, Reggie, I didn't really want a prize anyway!" she called after him. "But come on, we can go see the Axeman's show soon."

I moved closer, and Carl caught my eye, then grinned. I smiled back. Not the most reputable of games, but nothing that was taking money out of our pockets.

Rachel was getting hungry, so we swung by the food stands. Two of our men worked the charcoal grill, sweat running down their faces, while two young women from town took orders at the counter. Our guy Jake ran the cash box.

The aroma made my stomach queasy again, but Rachel liked hotdogs, so I took her around the back of the stand. One good thing about running the show—we didn't have to stand in line. But I made a point of paying for her hot dog even though I didn't have to. No point in encouraging people to help themselves to the food, if that was what was really happening.

We perched on a wooden box behind the big cooler where we'd be out of the way of the workers manning the charcoal grill. Rachel slowly nibbled away on her hot dog, getting ketchup on her face. I enjoyed just resting with her, even though I wasn't hungry.

We sat there so long that I was pretty sure the workers forgot we were there — they were so busy. My eyes started drifting shut when suddenly I jolted awake at a new voice behind the counter. The deep voice was familiar, but I couldn't place the speaker in my mind. Keeping low, I peeked around the edge of the cooler and saw a tall man standing in the cashier's place. He was taking some of the money out of the cash box!

I couldn't see his face clearly as we were behind him, but as he moved, the familiar mustache made me think it was Abe. When he turned to speak to one of the counter girls, though, I realized this fellow was Abe's brother, Jed, whom we had hired to work security at the carnival.

But it wasn't *his* job to take the money from the booths. Only Douglas was supposed to do that, and Abe was to collect the money from the ticket booth. However, none of the workers seemed distressed to see Jed with his hand in the cash box.

He must've convinced them all that this was regular procedure, using his position as Security Chief. These were mostly townies, not regular carnies, so it probably didn't even occur to them that he would trick them.

When nobody was looking, he shoved his hands deep down the front of his pants and stashed the money in what I suspected was a magician's pocket. I kept Rachel quiet until he was gone. After cleaning up her face as best I could, we snuck away out the back of the stall to meet Douglas.

Chapter Nine

I changed clothes, and we got to the big tent just in time for the performance.

Douglas paced up and down behind the entry curtain. "There you are! I was worried. Did you find out anything? I have an idea."

After nestling Rachel into her little spot on the quilt with her dolly, I hugged him and then whispered in his ear all the things we had seen.

"That fits!" His hands tightened on my shoulders. "I've been thinking about something I saw at the tavern when we were in town. Remember I said that Abe was in there and had a crowd with him? Well, our chief ticket-taker Harold was there with him, and they were acting mighty friendly. I felt a little funny at the time but didn't want to cast any aspersions."

The two of us peeked out the entryway at the other archway where Abe waited to go on later. We would have to confront him and his brother, but I sure didn't want to do that with all his axes around.

That night after the show, I carried the sleeping Rachel back to our room and tucked her into her little bed on the floor. Snuggling her rag doll next to her, I grabbed my cloak and tiptoed back out of the room. Douglas and I had to go scout around the fair some more, and I hoped Rachel would be fine for a little while on her own. I stopped with my hand on the doorknob for a long moment, then turned and headed out of the barn toward the ticket booth.

I skirted around the open area, walking along the tree line so that I wouldn't be so visible. I thanked my foresight in grabbing my black cloak as I pulled the hood up over my head to hide my red hair.

When I got to the end of the access road, I stopped under the trees and watched the ticket taker in his booth. Harold was the townie we'd hired to sell tickets in the hopes that locals would trust us more if they saw a familiar face at the gate. And we figured we could trust him because he was an accountant.

The main show was over, and it was unlikely that more people would come into the fair at that hour, so it seemed he was reconciling his money and numbers—even through the darkness, I saw his frowning face bent over the table in the booth by the light of the single bare bulb outside.

He had a pencil behind his ear, and I could hear coins clinking. It seemed to be taking him a long time, as all we ever asked him to do was turn over the money and the ticket count; we did the reconciliation ourselves. My suspicions were confirmed when I saw another figure striding toward the booth from the fair area. I recognize the tall, lanky frame—it was Abe.

He stepped up to the booth and greeted the ticket taker with a brotherly clasp around the shoulders. "How's it looking, buddy? How'd we do tonight?"

The ticket taker looked up, and the light from the single bulb showed his big grin. I couldn't hear his answer, but he passed a canvas bag over to Abe, and then they shook hands. Abe came out of the booth with what I now saw were two bags. He slipped one into a deep pocket down the front of his trousers just like his brother had done and arranged it so it increased the bulge in the front of his pants. I snorted silently to myself. Men.

Abe and Harold headed jauntily toward the fair area, having agreed to go grab a beer. The other canvas bag was under Abe's arm—the one he would give Douglas and tell him was the entire take for the night from the ticket booth.

Once they passed my spot, I scurried out along the tree line and headed back toward the barn to meet Douglas. He was already waiting for me inside. As I dashed in, out of breath, I threw my arms around his neck, and he hugged me back.

"Hey, hey! You okay?"

"Yes, I'm fine." I gasped for breath. "But you won't believe what I just saw. The ticket taker Harold gave Abe some of the money from tonight's gate!"

His hands tightened on my shoulders. "So, it's as we suspected. That bastard. They're all in on it together. But if it's one thing I know, carnies will not put up with people stealing from their own. He's not going to get away with this. Let me round up some of the boys. You all right with waiting here in case he shows up before I get back?"

At my nod, he slipped out the back of the barn, heading toward the midway.

I peeked in on Rachel, breathing a sigh of relief that she was still sound asleep, then quietly closed the door again. I sat down at my sewing machine and tried to look like I was busy with something as Douglas usually met Abe to get the money.

I hoped he wouldn't show up until Douglas was back, but my hopes were in vain—I heard a strong, confident set of footsteps approaching on the gravel outside the barn, and Abe opened one side of the double doors. He paused and looked around the empty barn, then his gaze went back to me. "You're here by yourself, missy?"

I tried to look confident. "Yes, I had some work to do on the machine here. Douglas said something came up that needed his attention and to tell you that he would be back in just a minute. Would you like to sit down?" I gestured toward one of the benches still left in the barn and inwardly rolled my eyes. I sounded like I was inviting him to sit down at a tea party, for crying out loud.

"Well, I don't mind if I do," he drawled as he pulled the bench over next to where I sat. A bit too close. I tried to calm my beating heart and hoped that Douglas would be back soon.

"I have to say, my brother and I are pretty glad that we found your little show here," he said as he leaned in toward me. "Folks have been quite friendly… if you know what I mean."

He put a hand on my arm, and I carefully pulled it away, my hand coming to rest on my belly. I saw his gaze follow my hand and inwardly cringed. Don't make him think about personal stuff.

A sense of relief flooded through me when I heard footsteps on the gravel outside. Douglas appeared, framed in the doorway for a moment. He looked at Abe and then me and seemed to take in the situation at a moment's glance.

"Well, Abe. Do you have tonight's receipts? I have to say that putting the man who could wield an axe so well in charge of picking up the ticket receipts seems to be a stroke of genius."

He stopped a few feet away from us and stood, feet apart, his arms crossed and his suspenders setting off his shoulders. Abe stood and faced him, topping him by at least three inches. But to his credit, Douglas didn't back down at all.

"So, the money?"

Abe pulled what looked like a sheepish face and held his hands out wide to each side. "I'm very sorry to have to tell you, boss, but somebody stole the money from the ticket taker. He said they took it all."

Douglas's eyes narrowed. "Really? Tonight. That's funny because that's not what he just said."

At his words, the other half of the barn's double doors opened. A dozen carnies and roustabouts stood outside. Two of our men flanked the ticket taker, twisting his arm behind his back. Harold looked everywhere but at Abe.

Jake and Nathan held Abe's brother Jed, the alleged security chief, by the arms. He was bleeding from his lip, and one eye was puffed closed. I had the feeling that if they let go, he would hit the ground.

Clearly, Jake had not taken kindly to the news that Jed had tricked him into allowing money to be skimmed from the cash box at the hot dog stand and had made his displeasure known.

Abe's face went pale. "Hey now, what have you done to my brother? How *dare* you?"

The two holding Jed dragged him over to stand next to his brother.

"The question is," — Douglas spit on the floor — "not what we've done to your brother, but what have *you* done to all of *us*? We trusted you to join this community and be part of what we were trying to do here. But the two of you have stolen from us. Stolen from me. Stolen from my wife and child and all that we are trying to do for our future."

I couldn't help myself. "And from our new baby on the way," I blurted out.

My husband's gaze flicked toward me, and I saw a huge smile break across his face for a moment, but he got right back to business.

"And you've stolen from our unborn child. You know that we carnies can't allow that."

Abe tried to bluster his way out of the situation, edging toward the exit, but three of the men came and stood between him and the door, facing the axeman.

"You're done here as of now," Douglas said. "Give me the money and tell me where the rest of it is."

Abe's hand shook a little as he tried to flick his hair back from his face. "There isn't any money left. I had to pay the people I owed, folks I borrowed from in the rough times. They've been following me and threatening us for a long time. That's why I took this job. They said they'd kill our mother."

"So that's why we've never heard of you in the carnie circuit. I have to say, you are a natural at it, buddy."

I cleared my throat and spoke softly to Douglas. "They stashed some of the money in the front of their pants."

The man nearest me must have heard as he stepped forward and rolled up his sleeve. "Are you going to get it, or am I?"

Abe quickly shoved his hand down the front of his pants, pulled out the canvas bag, and handed it over to my husband. Jed did the same. That was the money they had skimmed off the top of the till and likely wouldn't pay all our expenses—but it was better than nothing.

Douglas looked at the other men. "Let the ticket taker go. He's just a townie and doesn't understand. We don't want any bad feelings with the town over this. But take these two back to the tents to get their stuff and make sure they get out of here. Be sure to search for the money."

"Okay, boss," one of the carnies said. "But what's going to happen to the show now? He was the biggest draw. Everybody was coming to see him."

Douglas's lips tightened. "Well, we're just going to have to come up with a new attraction, that's all. And do it in a hurry." He turned away from the thief with a sneer of disgust. "Now, get him out of here. But no need to be gentle with him, if you know what I mean."

My eyebrows raised. I suspected that Abe would look worse than his brother by the time he got off carnival property. Two of the men escorted the ticket taker out the door toward the exit road, and the rest grabbed Abe and his brother by the elbows and hauled them off toward the tent village, being none too gentle as they went.

"Oh golly, honey. That was intense." I felt myself shiver as I stood next to Douglas.

He squeezed me in a tight embrace. "It was indeed. But"—he kissed my neck and then my lips, hungrily—"what's this about a new baby on the way?" He pulled back and smiled into my eyes.

I nodded, not sure of my voice. Took a deep breath. "I think so… I'm not quite sure yet. But this just makes it harder for us. I didn't want to add any pressure on you with the carnival and all, so I didn't tell you yet."

"I'm not worried. It's wonderful news. But now, we just need to figure out how to get an attraction going that will pull people in immediately. Something they've never seen before. Something they can't see anywhere else."

I looked at him, thinking furiously and trying to decide if I should tell him.

He went on, "What we really need is something special that'll attract a lot of attention. Like an animal act! P. T. Barnum always had the most amazing creatures in his shows. We just need a hook, and then we could promote it like crazy all week long."

I knew just the thing.

I pulled Douglas down to sit with me on the bench, our knees touching. I turned slightly toward him, my hands clasped in my lap. "Do you remember how you asked about my family in Scotland, dear?"

He nodded. "I'm so sorry I never got to meet any of them. You said your parents came over when you were a little girl, but they both died when you were young?"

"Yes, but there's more to it than just that, honey." I looked down at my hands, then firmed my lips and looked back at my husband.

"My parents had a special ability that came down through my mother's side. I think it could help us here. Would you be willing to keep an open mind?"

CHAPTER TEN

1969: SUNDAY, JUNE 8

Jane woke up with a start, her dreams still running through her head. She pictured a huge blue eye staring at her from the water, a circus tent, and a midway lit by bare bulbs against the night sky — then turned her head and saw her grandmother's diary resting against the pillow next to her head.

She sat up, frantically feeling all around with both hands, and relaxed when she saw the dried sprig of forget-me-nots lying safely on her nightstand. Tucking the flowers inside the diary, she smiled. "I'll have to read more of you later, Dear Diary, as Grandma would say. Today is church, and then I'm taking Marilyn to see the Falls."

Checking the clock, she jumped out of bed, got dressed, and headed downstairs for breakfast. The chalkboard in the kitchen confirmed that Rob was already at work at his busboy job, and Dad was at the construction site. Both said they'd be back by dinnertime.

Jane grabbed the phone receiver off the wall, held it against her ear with her shoulder while she dialed, then stretched the coiled cord across the kitchen while she popped some English muffins in the toaster. Marilyn's father answered the phone and then put her on.

"Hi, Jane! Are you guys okay after yesterday's crazy adventure? Still want to take me to see Niagara Falls?"

"You bet. Rob's at work at the diner today, and I have to go to church, but let's go after lunch."

"Cool. Hold on a sec." Marilyn had some quick words with her father, keeping the phone away from her for a moment. "My parents and I will pick you up around one o'clock, okay? He said they can sight-see on their own and then meet us later to drive us home."

"Awesome. Bring a camera if you have one. Dress warmly. And wear a raincoat!"

They hung up, and Jane headed out the door, munching on her muffin, hoping that all the butter wouldn't drip out of the nooks and crannies onto her mock turtleneck top.

Three hours later, the girls stood together at the American Falls Viewing Area, looking over the shoulder-high railing. It snaked around the platform, almost hanging over the water.

The cascading water directly in front of them captured their total attention as they stood at the level where the water went over the lip in an S-shaped curve. The two stood mesmerized by the power and majesty of the sight—both Marilyn, seeing it for the first time, and Jane, who had grown up seeing it yet never failed to marvel at the power of the Falls.

"So, what do you think?" Jane finally dragged her attention away to ask her new friend.

"What? Holy cow, that's loud!" Marilyn shook her head, grinning like crazy as occasional droplets sprayed their faces, then leaned in closer. "It's awesome! I've seen pictures but had no idea how overwhelming it would be up close like this. I can feel it in my bones!"

"Rob and I snuck out to see the Falls at 3:00 a.m. once. The view is even more intense at night when you can barely see it, but you can feel the rush and power of the river."

"Whoa! Did you get caught?" The California teen rolled her eyes. "My dad yelled at me once for going out to hear a midnight band. But it was worth it!"

Jane smiled in remembrance. "Yeah, but he didn't yell. I guess I'm not surprised because my dad always wants to work with water. Speaking of pictures, did you bring your camera?"

"Oh, yeah, I'm enjoying this so much I forgot." Marilyn dug in the pocket of her raincoat and pulled out an Instamatic. She carefully rested it on the railing and snapped a picture of the water. "Hold on, I want a picture of you with the Falls in the background!"

Jane posed in front of the Falls while Marilyn took her picture. "Okay, your turn!" She snapped a shot of her friend holding her fingers up in a peace sign and gave the camera back. "Cool!"

A bit farther along the railing, Jane noticed a large family doing much the same thing. It looked like three generations, with grandparents, parents, and teen children. She tried not to stare but was struck by the realization that her own family could have been doing this all together if her mother and grandmother had survived. She pressed her lips tight for a moment at the sudden emptiness she felt.

The family had a bit of trouble getting everyone arranged for the picture. It looked like they were trying to decide who should take the shot, and when Jane saw the grandmother move back with the camera to frame the rest of her family against the Falls, Jane stepped forward.

"Excuse me, but may I help? I'd be happy to take a picture of all of you!" She held out her hands for the camera.

The older woman turned to her, startled, but her face relaxed when she met Jane's gaze. "Oh, why yes. Thank you, dear!" She handed over the camera and insisted on telling Jane how to work it.

Jane suppressed a smile. It was the same kind of camera she had just used with Marilyn, but she allowed the grandmother to fuss over her for a moment and actually enjoyed the attention. The woman went to pose with the rest of her family. Jane made sure she could see everyone's faces, then snapped the picture. The grandmother came back to retrieve the camera and thanked her.

"It's okay, really," Jane said. "It's important that you be in the picture too! They will appreciate it someday."

The older woman gave her an odd glance for a moment, then shrugged and offered to take a picture of the two friends together. Marilyn passed her camera over with glee, and the two teens posed once more, this time with their arms around each other's shoulders and their cheeks pressed together. Marilyn thanked the lady, and Jane watched after the other family as they moved off down the walkway.

Marilyn turned to Jane. "Cool. I'll have Dad get an extra print made for you when he has them developed. Hey. Earth to Jane! You okay?" She waved her hand in front of Jane's face.

"Oh, yeah." Jane blinked a few times and dragged her attention back to her friend. "Just thinking about how different they are from my family... or how much the same we might have been. My family is so small now."

"Aww, Jane, I kinda know the feeling, but differently 'cus I'm an only child. I'm glad we're getting to be friends! We should get our families together for a barbecue or something this summer once your dad isn't so busy. Anyway, you wanna try this binocular thingy?"

Marilyn pulled a coin out of her pocket and shoved it in the nearest viewing machine on a post without waiting for an answer.

She turned the viewer back and forth across the Falls with her face pressed to the eyepiece. "Whoa, cool! So, why do I see more mist from the other side of the land there?"

Jane leaned in close to her friend to be heard. "Oh, that's Goat Island. Somebody used to keep a goat herd there in colonial times! It splits the river into two sections, and there's a waterfall on either side. The area we're seeing is called the American Falls, and it's the smaller of the two. On the other side of the island is Horseshoe Falls, on the Canadian side, and it's even bigger."

"What? You're kidding. This isn't even all of it? And what's that boat down there?" Marilyn pointed to what looked like a ferry boat packed with people, all wearing yellow, in the river at the bottom of the Falls.

"Yeah, it's cool from here, but it looks *amazing* when you see it from the Canadian side. And that's the *Maid of the Mist*. Next time we come back, we can bring Rob and George and take the boat ride now that we're not so scared of boats anymore. I remember from when I was little. You think there's a lot of spray up here? They give you a yellow slicker because you get *soaked* down there!"

She pointed out all the rock at the bottom of the Falls, explaining that it was called talus and was part of what her father's project was trying to take care of. It had fallen off the lip of the Falls years ago, but the water now landed on the talus instead of falling straight down to the river below like it used to.

Jane had a flash of what it would look like to be down at the bottom of the waterfall, looking up. She shivered and hugged herself for a moment.

After a while, the pair walked along the sidewalk of the viewing platform, heading upriver from the Falls. Jane never failed to be amazed at the churning mass of water as it roiled over the rocky riverbed. It both drew and repelled her. She told Marilyn that it was called Hell's Half Acre and that they were heading toward the area where her father was helping the construction company build the cofferdam at the tip of Goat Island.

"So, what's a cofferdam, anyway? It sounds like a coffin or something," Marilyn mused, eying the water. "And how on earth would you build a dam in *that*?"

Jane shivered at the words without knowing why. "From what my dad says, they're gonna dump something like twenty thousand tons of rock in a line from here to the island. Gonna take maybe three days, and then all the water will be cut off and diverted around the other side of Goat Island to the Horseshoe Falls. You know, the Canadian side."

Marilyn walked up ahead while Jane stopped and stared at the rushing water, looking back toward the American Falls with a sense of… what? Longing? What had her father mentioned about the family and the water? She still had more to read in the diary — and that made her think of her grandparents' carnival.

She looked back at the forest along the edge of Goat Island, smiling at a lone deer stepping out onto the rocky edge of the island for a drink. Suddenly, she shrieked as a large, dark shape reached out of the river and bit the deer around its neck, pulling it into the water! The deer bleated in panic, kicking its thin legs until it suddenly went limp in the creature's jaws just as it disappeared under the surface.

"What the hell!" Jane stood, staring in shock. She regained her composure enough to look around and see that nobody else was looking in that direction. Had she imagined it? Was her mind playing tricks on her? But no, the other deer were gathered in a group, urgently bleating.

Marilyn startled her by returning, saying that there just seemed to be a lot of construction stuff up ahead, and it was almost time to meet up with her parents. Jane was quite willing to go along with the suggestion and get away from… whatever she had just seen.

When they joined Marilyn's parents at the Collins' Mercury station wagon, Jane suggested they take a different way home and go down the Niagara Highway because her dad always said traffic was better. In truth, she was secretly pleased when they agreed and listened to her directions, being new to the area, as she had an ulterior motive.

As the two girls climbed into the rear-facing seats in the way back, Marilyn kept up a steady stream of chatter about how cool the Falls were and how much she was looking forward to seeing *Dark Shadows* the next day. Jane managed to keep up her end of the conversation, but she was also busy watching out the window.

After a bit, she interrupted Marilyn's description of how funny the latest Smothers Brothers show had been.

"Marilyn, look there! There it is. That's Fantasy Island. It's a cool carnival, with rides, and a midway, and games. My dad took us there a bunch of times. Maybe we could all go!"

She pressed her face to the glass as they went past the carnival, drinking in all the features she could see and trying to remember what it had been like to walk on the grounds. And she tried to picture how it would feel to run a carnival.

Suddenly, between the carnival and the strange feeling she had at the river, she wanted to get home and finish Emily's story.

Chapter Eleven

When we headed into town the next week, we were both a lot quieter than we had been on previous trips. My stomach was in knots — we were going to have to ask for credit on the next food order, as we could only pay for part of it because of the missing money.

Of course, the butcher shop was going to be the biggest expense again. I had one handmade sign tucked in my bag in hopes that he would at least let us post it in his shop, even if he turned down our full order.

I played a little game with Rachel as we drove, trying to count as many cows as we could on the way by.

"My cow!" She pointed at the field on the right. "Cow, cow!"

Her curiosity made me grin. "Okay, I see them. One, two, three cows. Very good!"

She was still bubbly and enthusiastic, clutching her doll as we came into the butcher shop. The butcher stood behind the counter, just staring at us as he chewed his cigar stub. I wondered if he ever lit it.

Douglas nodded at him in a friendly manner. "We'd like to place the same order again for the next two weekends."

The butcher nodded. "Heard you had a little trouble out there. Harold told us at the Elks meeting."

Harold — I was sort of surprised that the ticket taker guy from town would've told anybody about his part in stealing our money. My stomach clenched.

The butcher went on. "He said that axeman guy and his brother were taking advantage of everyone, including him. And then you got rid of them."

I relaxed a bit. It made sense that the townie would blame the carnie for everything.

Douglas sighed. "Yes. We made a mistake and trusted someone we shouldn't have. But he's gone, and I don't expect we will see him or his brother around here again anytime soon."

The butcher broke out in a big grin.

"Well, ya know, I can't say that's such a bad thing. Maybe my wife will stop going on and on about that fellow now." He even got a little twinkle in his eye. "So, you want to place the same order?"

Douglas stood with his mouth partly open for half a beat, then managed to turn that into a smile himself. "Yes, please, but I'm afraid we're a little short on money now. We can pay you part of it..." His voice trailed off for a moment, and then he firmed his lips and continued. "And we can pay the rest out of this weekend's gate receipts."

"You're asking for me to extend you credit?" The cigar wiggled up and down as the butcher chewed on it for a moment.

Douglas took a deep breath and nodded.

The cigar butt switched to the other side of the butcher's mouth. "You and your family have proven yourselves to be worthwhile people. I wasn't sure about you at first, being with the carnival and all, but sure, we can try it this once. I'll have the delivery sent out on Friday and the week after."

Douglas handed over as much money as we could spare from our stockpile. He extended his hand. The butcher paused a moment before reaching out and giving him a firm handshake.

"Thank you, sir. This can make all the difference for us." My husband beamed, then leaned in conspiratorially. "Can you tell people that we have an amazing new creature act coming in this weekend? Something the likes of which they have never seen before! And do you mind if we put up a sign in the window?"

I pulled the "See the AMAZING creature!" sign out of my bag and held it up.

The butcher guffawed. "Now, how did I know you were going to say that? Sure, sure, post your sign. I'll pass the word."

"Thank you, sir." Douglas propped the sign up by the window, then shepherded the two of us out the door with him. When we were out of eyesight of the butcher shop, he grabbed little Rachel up in a big hug and squeezed me around the waist with his other arm. "It worked! I didn't know if that was going to or not. But this'll make all the difference!"

Tears in my eyes, I hugged him back and kissed his cheek. "I think it had a lot to do with you, dear. You've proven yourself to be a decent partner in so many ways."

That got me a real kiss.

"Now, let's go put up all these signs you made," he said when we came up for air.

We pulled the small stack of the remaining papers out of the truck. I had a good feeling as I looked at one of the signs and grinned at the artwork I'd sketched: a view of the lake with a boat in the middle and something long wrapped around the back end of the boat. If that didn't get their attention, I don't know what would.

Two young men wearing work boots and worn pants passed us on the street, animatedly talking to each other. "I tell you, Rigby saw it from his rowboat. It was at least sixteen feet long! Whatever it was, it circled him three times and then dove away under the surface. Said it was the scariest thing he'd ever seen on the water."

The other fellow whacked him in the arm. "Come on, pal. That Rigby must've been seeing things. There ain't nothing like that in the lake. Unless it was a sturgeon."

"I'm just telling you what he said. And Davis saw it too!"

The pair continued down the street as we stood on the sidewalk, grinning at each other like a pair of nitwits. I was so glad I had shared my family secret with Douglas, and that he had decided to accept it!

We tacked flyers up on telephone poles and went around to various stores asking to put them in the window, offering tickets to the show if they seemed reluctant. Then we stood on the corner, handing flyers out to people as they walked by.

We decided to do the same thing as before, splitting up so that Douglas headed into the tavern and I took Rachel into the grocer. We did have enough money to pay for the rolls, and I sat Rachel down on one of the tall stools at the soda fountain next to another little girl. Douglas and I had decided it was worth spending some of our limited money for a milkshake—because we'd promised it to Rachel, plus it might give me a chance to talk to more people about the carnival.

A woman was seated there on the other side of her daughter. She had beautiful long curls swept off her face and pinned back in rolls, and I smiled at her as I sat down. I knew how long that look had taken to achieve.

I ordered our milkshake to share and then casually placed the last few of the signs on the counter in front of Rachel, as if I was just freeing up my hands. Rachel and the little girl started jabbering at each other about their dolls.

The mother leaned forward over her daughter and looked at the sign. "Is that about the new show at the circus? What's that a picture of in the water?"

"Oh, hello. Yes, there is an amazing new animal show at the carnival. Something from the water that people have never seen before."

I smiled inwardly. Never seen before was certainly the truth—at least not in this neck of the woods.

"Oh, my goodness!" The woman fanned herself with her hand and then took a sip of her soda. "Yes, I heard my neighbor talking about that thing in the water. It's really true?"

The young woman behind the counter gave us the milkshake with two straws and leaned forward to hear our words as well, her curly bobbed hair tucked behind her ear on one side. "Yes! Jimmy said that he was out fishing, and something came by that pushed a lot of fish in his direction. He caught three where he usually only catches one!"

She eyed the picture upside down, and I turned it around so she could see it better. Her eyes grew wide. "Is it scary?"

I shook my head. "I wouldn't say… scary, exactly. But it sure *is* exciting. You should come and see the show."

She looked up at me, her eyes shining. "I'm going to tell Jimmy to bring me this weekend. I can't wait to see it since he was so excited."

"That's great! Say, is it all right if I put this up in the window?" I grinned when she nodded.

Rachel took a big slurp of our milkshake. "This is yummy, Mommy."

I patted her hair. "You bet, honey. It sure is."

When we met up again with Douglas, he was beaming. "That was fun. I got to be all mysterious and dramatic at the tavern, and *two* guys bought me a drink. I hope I didn't keep you waiting too long."

I shook my head and told him about the conversation at the soda counter.

"That's great! And then, you wouldn't believe it, but that ticket guy Harold came in."

"Oh no, was that awkward?" I put my hand to my lips.

"No! He took me aside and thanked me for saving his reputation. Said he'd only done it to pay off the debt on his house. And then, he went on to tell everybody how great the carnival was and encouraged them to come to the show!"

I breathed a big sigh of relief. "Well, that's wonderful. I was worried he could have been bad-mouthing us to the townies. You know, we might have a chance at this yet."

Chapter Twelve

Showtime came way too soon, considering all the work we'd had to do in moving the show lakeside. We had all the benches set up on the rocky shore area, facing the harbor, with a bonfire on each side to light the part we were using as the main stage. Our truck was parked to one side, facing the water, with the band in the open back and some of the entertainers gathered on the other side as if they were backstage.

Douglas and I squeezed each other's hands while we waited for the audience to be seated, as it looked like a decent crowd. Thankfully, it was a clear evening since there was no time to move the tent.

This time, Louie was on one side of the open area, and Douglas and I were alone on the other — I had convinced one of the young girls from the food stall to stay with Rachel up at the barn.

"Looks like a full house!" I grinned and leaned forward to kiss my husband. "Go knock 'em dead, honey!"

He started the show the same way he always did, striking a great pose and promising an amazing evening of unsurpassed delights. "Welcome, welcome! *You* are the luckiest people in the state of New York. We have some amazing feats of derring-do for you to see tonight! And…" He waited for the drumroll that came in almost right on time, then leaned forward to speak to the crowd in a stage whisper.

"We've heard some rumors roundabouts here concerning something… *strange*… in the lake. Has anyone heard about that?" Some hoots and hollers from the crowd. He stood up straight. "Well, we have something new with your entertainment in mind. Something you've been hearing about. Something that *no one has ever seen*."

He stopped with his arms raised for emphasis, then swept his arm down, pointing across the crowd. "Something that *you* will be the first to see. But first, let me introduce my new partner in the ring. The fantastic" — he waited for the drumroll — "energetic" — he paused for the drumroll again — "Louis the Maaaaag-*ni*-fi-cent!"

Douglas backed toward me, holding his arm out to indicate Louis, who sprang out into the firelight doing three cartwheels in a row — no mean feat on the rocky ground — and landed strong, standing tall with his arms raised over his head as the crowd cheered. He waited until the noise died down.

"Hello, hello, one and all! The first act we have for you tonight will amaze and astound you. May I present, Sebastian the Sword-Swallower!"

When the first act came out, Louis stepped back off the other side. Douglas slipped past me in the darkness and headed toward the far side of the rocky shore. I was pretty sure everyone's eyes were on the sword swallower and not watching him. He disappeared into the trees and out of my sight.

That was my cue. I followed behind him and stepped onto the rowboat at the small dock. Untying it, I dipped the oars in the water, making as little noise or splashing as possible. It was hard to tell when I got in the right spot since we had only practiced it once.

I looked back toward the shore and could see that I was centered between the two bonfires on each side of the stage area and about a hundred yards out. I pulled the oars into the boat and watched the water.

The wind held quiet, and we'd situated the stage at the edge of the harbor, so the water's surface remained fairly smooth. I peered across the water, rubbing my hands together with nerves. Two small, darkened lanterns sat at my feet.

My heart leaped when I saw a ripple on the surface heading toward me in the boat. I lifted the lanterns up and carefully hooked them onto the poles we had rigged onto the bow and stern of the boat, turning up the wicks and removing the coverings.

The last official act was just coming to an end. I heard the crowd burst into applause, and Louis took center stage again. But as he walked out from the sidelines, he stopped. With his large top hat on, it was easy to see him turn his head toward the water as if he were glancing in my direction, then do an exaggerated double take. He leaned forward and held one hand over his brow as if it would help him see better in the darkness.

The crowd started muttering — it was amazing how well the sound carried across the water. I hoped the timing would work, as I'd feel really stupid if I were just sitting out in the lake in a boat and nothing happened.

The ripple that had been approaching me drew nearer. Small waves disrupted the surface as it went back and forth beside the boat.

Louis swung his arm in a sweeping gesture at the water. "Ladies and gentlemen! Do you see what I see out there? There's a young lady in a boat! But… I don't know what to make of this…" He craned his head back and forth, peering at the water as he walked along the shore. He turned toward the audience.

"What on earth is in the water?" He pointed at the lake. "It looks like she's in danger!"

A woman in the audience squealed. Others started talking more loudly.

Louis put one finger to his lips and held up the other hand, and they quieted. "I can't see very well," he said. "Can you see? We need some light!"

A plant in the crowd yelled out, "Turn on the lights in the truck!"

I saw Louis throw up his hands and roll his head skyward as if that was the smartest thing he had ever heard.

"Lights, please, gentlemen," he asked the band. The piano player, who didn't have much to do anyway since we hadn't been able to move the piano to the water, jumped in the truck and turned on the headlights.

I was pinned by the high beams and raised an arm to block the light from my eyes. The rippling disturbance in the water grew stronger and started circling the boat. Despite myself, I dropped my arm and grabbed onto both of the gunwales to steady myself as the craft rocked.

The waves now came strong enough that the boat dipped in the water even though there was no breeze. It wasn't hard to make my body rock back and forth, swaying as if I was being tossed around even harder.

Louis called out from the shore. "Hold on, miss! Hold on!"

People in the crowd stood, some approaching the water. Louis held up both hands to keep them back. "Hold on, folks. We don't know what it is—or what will set it off!"

People muttered and sat back down. But nobody stopped watching!

I heard another sound from the shore and was momentarily confused until I realized that the drummer had started a long drumroll, slowly building in speed.

"I don't know if we'll be able to see what it is!" Louis called.

That was my signal. I grabbed the oar on the far side of the boat, away from the shore and the crowd, and tapped it three times on the floor of the rowboat. The disruption in the water had been circling around the boat. The next time it passed between me and the shore, something broke the surface!

All I saw in the light of the lanterns and the truck's headlights was a large shape at the front end, and then a long, sinuous body arcing out of the water and diving back down under. It continued for at least five seconds, the fin along the top of the back fluttering as it dove back under the surface.

The crowd went wild. Some people ran away from the beach, while others tried to get closer, but a few of the men had been waiting by the truck and ran out to stop people from going into the lake.

"Please, ladies and gentlemen, for public safety, take your seats! We don't want to provoke the creature." Louis got them under control in a few minutes, and I sat quietly as the creature stopped rocking the boat.

"Now folks, was I right or was I right? Have you ever seen anything like that before?" Cheers from the remaining crowd.

Louis called to me from the shore. "Miss! Are you all right?" I took a deep breath, then nodded and waved.

He turned back to the people on the benches. "You know, I've heard about something like this in a lake in the Scottish Highlands. Someone even got a picture of it a few years ago. They called it the Loch Ness monster. Well, we seem to have our own version here, near Buffalo, and I name it… *Bessie!*" The audience burst out into wild cheers.

Louis turned back to face me, cupping both hands around his mouth. "Hey, you! Bessie! Leave the young lady alone!"

My cue, again. I tapped twice with the oar. The thing causing all the commotion sped by with one final pass, swirling the boat around and flicking its tail out of the water as it dove deep beneath the surface and disappeared.

The remaining audience burst into applause and cheers. I unlocked the oars and dipped them into the water, pulling slowly toward the dock. Louis directed two of the men over to meet me. They helped tie up the rowboat and gave me a hand to step out. Together the three of us walked up to the shore; I curtsied, and they each took a deep bow.

The crowd went berserk! The carnival was saved. I was sure every single person there was going to tell all their friends!

I stood at the water's edge later that night, hands clasped together over my heart. "Come back to me, come back from the sea. Come back to me, our love will always be!"

I stared into the dark water. A ripple broke the surface far out in the harbor, and I bounced up and down on tiptoe.

"Come in. I've missed you!"

The ripples spread across the surface, leaving a V-shape in the water. It headed directly toward where I stood in front of the benches. I looked up and down the rocky shore and nodded to myself that nobody was nearby. Turning back to the water, I didn't flinch as a smooth round shape broke the surface, and I clapped my hands in appreciation.

"You did it! You're so much bigger than the last time."

The head reared up out of the water — not standing, like a man, but like a dog's head held up on the end of a tubular body. A long fluttering fin ran down its back like an eel. Gills flared open and closed on the side of the neck below the head while the massive face contorted. A large, racking cough shook the creature's body until it drew in a shuddering breath.

Despite myself, I took a step back on the shore. "Can you hear me?"

The creature's face morphed before me. The long, pointed snout retracted into a more human-looking shape. The narrow shoulders that supported the two arms of the creature broadened from being slim and in line with the long, sinuous body to those of a man. He reached up and wiped his face, holding out his arms for balance as the lower part of his body writhed in the water, then stood straight up.

"Hello, sweetie." Douglas's voice sounded hoarse, and he cleared his throat. "I guess I did it, right?"

"I'll say you did! That was amazing. I remember seeing my father transform when I was a girl, but after the first time, I didn't know if we could get it all right. Here," — I held out the towel draped over my shoulders — "I brought this for you. Are you cold?"

He walked out of the waist-deep water toward me, naked and shivering a bit in the late-night air. "I don't even know what I feel, to tell you the truth, but that was amazing. It was so exhilarating, darling! I swam under the water, and I could breathe! I could go so fast. Oh, I wish you could do it too."

I gave a small smile. "Yes, but if I change, there's nobody to call me back."

"I know, I know. Thank you for letting me do it. Never in a million years would I have thought I could do this."

"Did anybody see you?"

He rubbed himself all over with the towel and wrapped it around his waist. I'd fetched his clothes from where he left them on the water's edge and passed over his overcoat from the rocky beach behind us.

He shook his head as he slipped it on. "I don't think so. I did go by a boat out there. Well, I kind of had a little race with it. I wanted to see how fast I could go. And I beat it!"

"Did they see much of you?" I grabbed his arm. "We have to be careful at first. Just a tease."

"I think they did. But I understand, we need to do this with a plan. We want to be very careful how we attract attention here."

"Yes, because soon we're going to bill you as the Greatest Show on Water! And pack them in by the Fourth of July!" We both giggled, and he gave me a big hug as we walked through the dark, silent midway toward our room at the back of the barn.

Chapter Thirteen

We were coming up on Labor Day, which would traditionally be the last show for the summer. It gets cold on Lake Erie as soon as the leaves start to turn, and folks would stop coming to the carnival.

Douglas and I sat at our table, ledger book in front of us. I tapped the paper with my pencil as I reviewed the numbers. Despite the thefts, we'd had a very good summer — much better than we had even anticipated after the rough times. We could chalk that all up to Bessie.

I frowned as I looked over some of the recent entries and tapped my pencil faster. "I'm not sure why this amount isn't larger —"

Douglas reached out and stopped my tapping with his hand. "Darling, can we take a break for a minute?"

I looked at him in surprise. "But we seem to be missing —"

He smirked and got a little pink in the cheeks. Then he got down on one knee next to me, fumbling around in his pocket.

I giggled at him. "What are you doing? Are you going to propose? We're already married!"

The pink color grew more pronounced. "I know but hear me out. I've always been sad that I couldn't afford to give you a wedding ring. Remember when I went into town a few days ago to get a new part for the truck? Well, I also went to one of the shops there."

He pulled his hand out of his pocket with something clenched tight in his fist. "Darling, I love you. If you had to do it again, would you still marry me?"

He opened his palm, and there was a beautiful little gold band. He tossed the ring up in the air, caught it in two fingers, and held it up with a flourish so that it winked at me in the light from the lantern. Then he pulled a little sprig of forget-me-not out of his pocket and held it up.

I grabbed the flowers and threw my arms around his neck. "Oh honey, of course, I would. I love you, and I love our life. No matter what happens, we'll always remember each other." Pulling back, I planted a kiss on his lips.

He tilted his head to one side and gave a small smile. "You know, that's what I had engraved in it."

He gave me a peek inside the ring, which brought tears to my eyes, and then he slipped it on my finger. It was a little tight but felt fine once we got it over the knuckle. It made me happy because I knew it would never fall off.

"I'm going to wear it forever!" And I threw my arms around his neck again.

"Shhh! You'll wake up Rachel!"

MONDAY, SEPTEMBER 4, 1939

It was finally Labor Day. I stood at the edge of the rocky shore, waiting for my cue to head out into the water for the final show of the season. Douglas was already off the stage. In the two months since we'd started the water show, we had perfected the new venue—the roustabouts had moved the tent to cover the area by the water, and now we did the whole show there. We had even put gravel on the path that led to the shore.

Looking out over the crowd, I didn't see a single empty spot on the benches. Douglas—or *Bessie*—had saved the show.

I slipped into the boat and rowed my way out into position. There was a bit of a breeze, making some slight waves, and I had to scull a little bit to keep in the right spot without getting pushed downwind. But it would be all right—we'd been able to practice the show in different conditions. Douglas knew where to find me.

Louie had changed things up a little bit too. Now, as he emceed, he no longer pretended that he was seeing me for the first time. By the time the rest of the show wound down, everybody had started looking out into the water to see if they could spot us. Word-of-mouth is a powerful thing!

The emcee turned toward the water and pointed. "There she is! Right on time. I wonder if she'll have a visitor?"

The drummer started a long drumroll, and the truck's headlights flared on. I pulled the oars inside the boat and tapped on the floor for

Douglas's cue. He swam between the boat and the shore at just the right time.

A little girl in the audience squealed. "There's Bessie! Mommy, Mommy, I see Bessie!" The crowd chuckled and applauded.

Douglas swam around my boat in faster and faster circles, making it rock back and forth again as we did in the first show. But we knew that the audience would want more each time, so we had to turn up the juice. On this show, our last of the season, he jumped out of the water much sooner than he had done the last time.

The crowd went wild. People cheered, and lots of kids held up the little Bessie sock toys attached to a stick that we sold on the midway. I giggled at the thought of kids taking their sock toys home to sleep with a sea monster—when I knew I'd be sleeping with mine.

What was that sound? My head snapped up—it wasn't Douglas in the water, and it wasn't the drummer or any of the people or shore. It was a low throbbing. I scanned the water to see if I could pinpoint the source.

It seemed to be coming from Lake Erie, just beyond our harbor. As I turned my head and peered into the darkness, the noise grew stronger. It was a boat motor. No, it was multiple boats heading in our direction.

I scraped the oar across the bottom of the boat, making a long scree sound, my signal to Douglas that something unusual was afoot. He slowed down at the edge of the boat on one of his circles and rolled onto his side. I saw the large eye under the water staring at me, and I jerked a thumb over my shoulder toward the boats coming from the lake. He bobbed his head and dove under the water.

I didn't know why they were coming, but with luck, we could finish the show and get out of the way before we were disrupted by their noise. The sound of their motors grew stronger every minute, and now I could see four boats coming toward us with their fishing lights on. They were spread out in a line coming in from the opening of the harbor.

The emcee continued his shtick and cried out, "Is she in danger? Or is it friendly?"

Tapping the boat, I braced myself for the new part that we'd added to the act.

Douglas, aka Bessie, circled twice and built up a lot of speed, then turned and headed right at the boat. Just as it looked like he was going to ram me, he gave a giant twitch of the back end of his body and leaped out of the water. The long, sinuous body of a giant sea serpent arced over the boat, droplets of water spraying in every direction and soaking me as he hung in the air.

The crowd went berserk. It seemed to take many long seconds for him to go over the boat—we had practiced it, but it still unnerved me. At the end, he gave an unfortunate last twitch to thrust himself fully out of the water, and his tail banged into the back into the boat, which sent me spiraling toward the shore.

As I pulled out the oars to try and stop my progress, I looked up and saw that the fishing boats were almost on us. They did indeed have their lights on. A fishing net hung between each, linking them together. It was like they were trawling the harbor. What could they be hoping to catch?

Of course. How could I be so stupid? All the attention that we had gotten from the audience who came to our show must have attracted people who wanted to catch the sea monster. They wanted to catch Bessie—my Douglas.

I couldn't think of any way to help him. What could I do? I slammed the oars on the boat's edge in our abort signal and then pulled my way toward shore, hoping that he had seen the boats. He must have heard them in the water.

I saw his usual V-shaped ripple, made whenever he came to the surface, heading diagonally across the harbor—the wake rippled in the headlights from the truck on shore. He was trying to go to the far side of them, but it didn't seem like there was going to be room. The boats were covering the entire area of the harbor—they were going to catch him in their net.

His head broke the surface, and I saw him pause, then turn and make for the opposite side of the harbor, but he was running out of room where he could maneuver. I was almost at the dock, and he was getting pushed closer and closer to shore. They were either going to catch him in the net or force him onto the land.

I had a stroke of what I hoped was genius. Using the oar, I made the same signal on the boat that I had used to tell him it was time to do the final leap over me. I paused and repeated it. Watching his rippled wake and its reflection in the lights, I held my breath and saw him turn toward the boats. He sped up, faster than I had seen him go before. He aimed between the two center ones, his head above the surface as he came almost parallel with them. There was a huge convulsion in the water as the giant sea serpent leaped up and over the edge of the net that hung between the two boats. It seemed to take forever as his enormous body passed above them.

I felt like I lived an entire lifetime as he hung suspended in the air.

A giant splash told us that he had reentered the water on the other side—did he make it? Or did he get trapped in the nets trailing the boats?

The water behind the fishing boats was calm since the boats themselves slowed as they neared the shore. I glanced back to see that I was almost at the dock, then heard a huge roar from the crowd. Looking up, I realized that the people were shrieking; some were covering their eyes, and some were on their feet, pointing at the water.

I turned back to where Douglas had disappeared into the harbor. Farther out, closer to Lake Erie itself, a giant spot of turbulence arose in the water. It was Douglas! He made one circle, arced out of the water, and dove back underneath, with his V-shaped wake heading directly toward the lake. They would never catch him there. I could call him back later.

Suddenly intense cramps wracked my abdomen, and I doubled over. No! It was way too early. I couldn't lose the baby!

For so many reasons, this would be our last show.

Chapter Fourteen

Jane put the diary down when she finished and stared at the dried forget-me-nots that had been inside the cover. She tucked them back into place, her lips quivering, and tied the book up again with the faded pink ribbon. Heading from her reading chair into the kitchen, she found her father and Rob were home and already finishing dinner at the table.

"Hey there, Sis. We tried calling you for dinner, but I don't think you heard us." Rob took his last bite of burger. "I guess you were busy reading, huh?"

She slid into her chair. "Grandma Emily was a really good story-teller. I guess I did get sucked right into the story."

Dad got up and brought her a plate with a hamburger and green beans. She nodded her thanks as he slid it in front of her, and immediately took a huge bite.

He squeezed her shoulder as he sat down again. "Well, she and Grandpa were professional entertainers, after all. What did you think about the story?"

She put down the burger and swallowed the bite she'd been chewing. "Pretty amazing, actually. I'm not sure if I believe it all… except for what we've seen from the boat recently." She summed up the story in the diary for Rob, ending with, "You're going to want to read this too, but I just hit the high points for you."

Rob sat with his mouth open, staring at her.

"I don't get it. So… Grandpa was a mermaid?" Rob shook his head. "No way, I remember Grandpa, and we have pictures in the photo album. He didn't have a tail or anything. Are you making this up?" He sat back in his chair with his arms crossed.

Their father sighed. "No, not a mermaid, not a merman, but something that could live underwater. At the top of the food chain, too.

But it took two of them. Grandma Emily had to stay on the land, and she gave Grandpa Douglas the ability to transform. But the only way he could change back was if the woman he loved, someone from the family, was waiting for him on the shore and called him back."

Jane's mind was racing. "Okay, so you're telling us that it's true Grandpa turned into some aquatic creature a long time ago. And we grew up knowing that Grandma disappeared. Where's Grandpa?"

"Hon, he's still in Lake Erie. That's why we stayed in this area after your mom passed. And why I kept working on the water with the hydroelectric program, even though…" A sob escaped his lips. "Even though I wanted nothing to do with the water after your mom drowned."

Tears shone in his eyes. Jane slipped out of her seat and wrapped her arms around his neck. After a moment, Rob joined them in a family hug. A long pause followed, then the twins sat down and stared at their father, waiting for him to recover.

"To start, I'm glad you kids were both ready to hear the story." Edward frowned. "It's been very hard for me to talk about, to be honest. Losing Rachel was one of the hardest things in my life."

Jane could only imagine how tough it was for her father—and now understood even more about why. The two siblings had talked about their mother's loss a lot over the years, but every time they brought it up to their father, he somehow managed to change the subject.

"We know, Dad." She gave a tight smile. "And we know it wasn't easy raising us as a single parent. Especially two of us. But I feel like there's a lot of things from that day that we don't remember. What actually happened?"

Rob leaned forward too—his forehead creased with a frown.

Edward took a deep breath. "Well, okay, that day on the boat. It was a beautiful afternoon, and we enjoyed being out on the water. Your mom and I, the two of you… And Grandpa Douglas and Grandma Emily as well."

Jane sat back in surprise. She hadn't even remembered their grandparents being there that day and looked at Rob, who shrugged. Apparently, he didn't either. But Dad's words tickled something in her head.

"You see, it was the first time I had changed during the daytime," their dad said.

"Hold on. You change too?" Rob pushed back from the table, his face contorted in a scowl. "Are you telling me that you are... what, the Loch Ness monster? And you sank the boat, and then Mom and Grandma..."

"No, *no*, son. It wasn't like that. Your Grandpa Douglas had been teaching me some things about surviving in the water with boats around, which is why we were out in the daylight when there was some traffic. And some jerk in a hot speedster saw us and tried to chase us. He wound up swamping the boat you were all in."

Their father lowered his head. "Grandpa and I tried to save all of you, but there were boats and people all around. Your mom swam fine and insisted we take you kids first, and she would stay with Grandma. We brought you two to the shore, but when we got back... the boat had sunk."

Jane grabbed Rob's hand. "And that was when Mom...?"

"At first, both Mom and Grandma Emily were just... gone." Dad exhaled and seemed to diminish in his chair. "We looked and looked, and found your mother, washed downstream toward the Falls. She was holding onto a rock in the river."

"Was she...?" Jane's words choked in her throat.

He looked up at them, tears rolling down his cheeks. "Your mom must have known she was in bad shape. She changed me back while we were both in the water. I swam hard and pulled her to shore, but it was too late."

"What about Grandma?" Jane asked in a whisper. Rob squeezed her hand so hard the fingers were numb, but she barely noticed.

"The county Marine Unit arrived to help. Of course, we couldn't let them see Grandpa as a sea serpent. They searched for a day and a half, but never found Grandma."

Rob scraped his chair back and jumped up. "No, seriously. This is too much. Our relatives are... what, sea serpents? And Grandpa let Grandma drown? She was my *favorite*." He wrung his hands together, then turned and bolted from the room.

Jane could hear him pounding up the steps. His bedroom door slammed, followed moments later by the muffled strains of "The Sound of Silence" on his record player.

Edward shook his head. "He's gonna play that over and over again."

"Yeah, but it helps him calm down. He'll feel better after he gets to read the diary. I'll take it up to him in a little while."

Her father rumpled her hair as he used to when she was little. "You know, sometimes I think you're both his sister and his mother. So, anything else you want to ask about?"

"Aaaw, thanks, Dad. Okay, so I get that it takes a woman of the family to call the man back from the water. So, with Grandma gone, what's going on with Grandpa?"

"He's still out there. In the water." He stared at the floor, then looked up at her. "He's been out there for ten years."

She gasped. "All by himself?"

"Yes. I've been watching the newspapers all along, and he's been sighted a few times. Once in 1960, down in Sandusky, on the south shore of Lake Erie. A man said he was out fishing on a clear, calm night and started to throw rocks at some rats he heard, when he saw… something…" — he gave a big sigh, then went on — "something that looked like a giant cigar that rose up out of the water a couple of feet."

"Can't you… can't you *do* anything?"

He shook his head. "Believe me, I've tried. That's why we're still here in this area, even though I would have loved to move away, far away from the water and where it all happened. But I can't just leave him there alone. And I've tried. I've tried so hard, but I don't have the ability to call him back."

"It's only the women who can recall them?" She tapped her finger on her lips.

He nodded. "A woman who loves the man very much can call him back." His glance flickered at her and then away. "So, I don't know what to think."

"Maybe I can do it."

A few hours later, Jane stood outside Rob's door, listening to the quiet sounds of Simon and Garfunkel. With luck, that meant he was calming down. She tapped gently, holding the diary clutched to her chest.

A moment later, she heard his quiet voice. "You might as well come on in."

She opened the door and stepped inside. He lay on his bed in the semi-darkness. The blue lava lamp that burbled and morphed on his desk cast weird blue shadows around the room.

"Kind of looks like the water, doesn't it?" he asked, staring at the ceiling. "Is this why I've always liked it? *Is it true?*"

Jane sat down on the foot of his bed. "I don't know. We're both Mom's kids, and if she had this ability, as did Grandma..."

"I don't know what to think. But it's like, ever since the accident, something... something wants me... *us*, there."

She nodded. "Now I understand what it is." She put the diary in his hands.

Chapter Fifteen

1969: Monday, June 9

A delightful aroma tickled her nostrils. Jane rubbed her face with her hand, still floating on the cloud of sleep. Then her eyes snapped open, and she remembered all the conversations from the night before. Her heart hammered in her chest, but that wonderful aroma helped calm her down. A few minutes later, she followed her nose down the stairs.

Coming into the kitchen, she saw her father at the stove flipping pancakes. A huge pan of bacon bubbled away on the other side, and the TV played the early morning news.

She paused at the doorway. "Dad! You made breakfast? On a Monday?"

"I just feel bad because I've been so busy with the work project. That damned dam." He turned to look at her. "And in the middle of all this stuff about the family, no less. Get any sleep?"

Jane shrugged. "I guess so because I don't remember being awake all night, but I can't say as I feel rested. Seen any sign of Rob yet?"

Her father shook his head as he pulled plates out of the cabinet.

She opened the silverware drawer, grabbed enough for the three of them, and set the table. "He was pretty upset last night, Dad. I gave him the diary to read. I hope that helped."

Her father paused at the stove with his chin on his chest. Then he firmed his shoulders and started moving pancakes onto a platter. "I hope so too, hon. I have to say, I didn't know what a strange family I was marrying into. But it probably wouldn't have made a difference… I loved your mother so much."

"Bacon." Rob stumbled into the kitchen, rubbing his eyes.

Edward grinned. "Coming right up, bud." He plopped a large plateful of bacon in the middle of the table. "Coffee's on, too."

Rob filled a cup and added some cream. "This almost makes me feel like the world is normal, you know?" He sort of hugged himself with his arms as he slid into the chair, his body tight. "Thanks, Dad."

Their father sat in the seat between the two siblings and reached out to put a hand on each of their shoulders. "I need to tell you again how sorry I am that this all happened to you two. It was never our intention to make your life strange or weird. Then after Rachel passed... I just didn't know when to start telling you guys about it. And nobody else knew."

"It's okay, Dad," Rob said. "I read the diary last night. I was up late, but I felt better after I was done. I'd thought they were just, I don't know, weird sea monsters. But reading the diary made me feel like they were real people, with hopes and dreams—"

"Yes, oh yes!" Jane chimed in. "I'm so glad you read it, Rob. But now, what do we do going forward? It seems like Grandpa, or Bessie, is making a presence again, right, Dad?"

Edward nodded. "I was trying to think of why that was. I've been trying to stay in touch with him for these ten years as best I can. I get out on Lake Erie or the river as much as I can for work, and sometimes he comes by, but I never know when he'll be there or not. But it seems like he came right to the boat you two were on, right?"

She nodded. "Yes, I saw that same V-shaped wake that Grandma Emily mentioned in the diary. It was coming straight across Lake Erie toward us. Like something was calling it."

"Well, did you get in the water or anything? I know from my brief experience that I could hear things better under there and could even smell things in the water, too."

Jane's eyes widened. "Yes! I was trailing my fingers in the water when we went out in the boat the first time. And then the second time, as well."

"Do you think Grandpa *smelled* you in the water and came to find you?" Rob stared at her. "Wait, you were wearing George's jeans jacket for a while. Didn't you say it... Bessie... pulled it into the water?"

"Whoa. That's right. Bessie was already there and pulled the jacket off the gunwale after it went partly in the water."

Rob turned to their father. "Dad, could he be drawn to her scent because she's a female member of the family?"

The older man stroked his chin and nodded. "I'd say that's a pretty good possibility." He shook his head. "Otherwise, I don't know why he would be up at this end of the lake in the daytime. I wonder if he needs something. We'll have to think. But first, bacon."

It didn't take long for them to polish off their breakfast. When they were done, their dad pushed his plate away and leaned back in the chair. "Same deal, right? I cook, you clean."

Rob grinned. "Okay, my turn." He took the plates over and started rinsing them off. "So, why do you think Grandpa was coming to find Jane?"

"I have no idea. But it could well be that he's lonely. Or maybe something about Jane's scent reminded him of Grandma Emily, and he was drawn to it?" Their father shrugged.

"So. What are we going to do about it?" Jane tapped her finger on the table.

"I'm not sure there's much we can do, kids. But today, you guys have school, and I have a long day at work. We're starting to dump the rocks in the water to dam off the east fork of Niagara. Afraid I'm not gonna be home much in the next few days."

Chapter Sixteen

1969: Wednesday, June 11

Jane came downstairs in the morning, surprised to see her dad in the kitchen with a cup of coffee. Two days had passed in a blur of school and homework. She and Rob had barely seen their father, as he had been working fifteen-hour shifts during the construction of the dam and was gone before they got up, only getting home in time to eat and fall into bed for a few hours.

He looked haggard and worn but was smiling.

"Hey! How goes the dam building, oh senior beaver?" She pulled up her upper lip, showing her front teeth, and pretended to be gnawing away at a log.

"Amazing. We've dumped almost a thousand truckloads of rock into the river so far. I don't have to go in until this afternoon because we're just going to keep working all night to finish tomorrow."

"Cool, Dad!" Rob said as he stumbled into the kitchen and flicked on the little black-and-white television out of habit, adjusting the antenna tipped with aluminum foil until the picture sharpened. A news broadcast was airing, and they caught a quick glimpse of a shot of the water.

Jane pointed. "Look! That's near the marina where we were with George, isn't it?" They all peered at the little screen, which showed a Utica Club billboard in the background. *No artificial bubbles! We age beer the natural way.*

"Holy cow, you're right. Isn't that by the parking lot?" Rob moved closer to the set.

The voiceover came on. "While progress on the cofferdam has continued, several pleasure boaters have reported seeing something unusual in the water a bit upstream. We brought a team out to look but can't say that we discovered anything specific. There was, however, some unusual turbulence."

The camera zoomed in on the reporter, standing by the river's edge and holding a microphone. "Is something down there? Could it be Bessie, the sea serpent, reported in the area thirty years ago? I'll talk with residents who remember those days at the dinner hour."

The three stared at each other. Jane was the first to speak. "Holy crap. I guess that answers the question of whether we need to do something. If people are reporting it to the news, and they're investigating, it's just a matter of time before somebody finds Grandpa. Right?"

Edward nodded. "Okay, kids. How about you skip school and come out onto the water with me this morning? I don't want to get too close to the dam construction as someone might see us. We need a boat. Rob, do you think George and his family would let us borrow theirs?" He leaned forward as Jane started shaking her head and put his hand on hers.

"No worries, hon, I can drive the boat, and you can wear a life vest. Are you kids in?"

Rob came over and stood between the two of them. "We're in. Let me call George for the boat keys before he leaves for school."

An hour later, the three met George at the marina. He said the boat was gassed up and reviewed all the things they would need to know about the craft.

Edward listened, then accepted the key the teen passed over and shook his hand. "Thank you so much for meeting us here and loaning us the boat, George, but seriously, you should be in school."

"No worries! I'm a senior. Not much left to do for the rest of the school year. I'm just looking forward to getting away to college!" His grin was infectious, and Jane and Rob smiled back.

"Man, you are going to get into so much trouble when you're away." Rob shook his head.

Their friend sobered a moment. "Are you sure you don't want me to go out with you? I mean, I trust you with the boat and all, but I thought maybe it would help. We've seen some weird stuff out there."

The twins looked at each other. Jane wasn't sure how to turn him down — after all, it was his boat. But the thought of explaining their family secret to someone, even a good friend, filled her with dread.

Edward smiled and shook his head. "No, but thanks, George. Let's just say this is the next step on getting these two more reconciled to the water, and it should be just a family affair."

George nodded. "I dig it. Okay, have a good day, and Rob, I'll get the keys from you later. No point in telling my parents I didn't spend the day with you." He looked sharply at Edward, then gave a shrug and grinned.

Jane breathed a sigh of relief as George waved on his way to the car.

The family headed for the dock where George's boat was kept. Edward carried a small duffel bag over his shoulder. He flashed a smile and waved as they passed the marina attendant who was out doing some sort of repair on one of the other docks — although he had a lawn chair out there as well and had been dozing in the sun when they arrived. The man tipped his hat at them, having watched them talk with George.

The three walked along the dock, looking at the water on either side, which reflected the morning sunlight in a brilliant sheen. The marina was deserted, being a weekday. As they neared the little boat at the end of the dock, they paused.

"Okay, does anybody have a plan here?" Rob stood with his shoulders hunched and his hands in the pockets of his denim shorts. He shivered a bit in the breeze. "I mean, what do you usually do when you come out here, Dad? I don't know, do you sing to him or what?"

Their dad smiled. "Oh, trust me. Nobody would come if I sang. You've heard me in the shower, right?"

That got the teens to giggle.

Edward passed the duffel to Rob. "Let's just get out on the water and see what happens. Maybe he'll sense us, or at least Jane. It seems like he's been hanging around this area, according to the news."

The twins paused a moment, then looked at each other and shrugged. They took a deep breath and went aboard. Jane distributed the life vests while their father untied the boat and started the engine; they were soon underway. Jane rejoiced that despite their initial apprehension, she and Rob were both a lot more comfortable on the boat. Rob took his usual seat next to the driver, and she moved about the boat carefully, looking it over and trying to formulate a plan.

Edward headed out into the river and turned upstream toward Lake Erie as the twins told him they had done before. He paused at a wide spot in the river and put the outboard motor in idle.

Jane tapped the ladder that led off the back of the boat with her foot. "Dad, is this thing safe? I was thinking that since Grandpa, or Bessie, or whatever we want to call him, came toward me when I touched the water before, what if I went down the ladder?"

Edward nodded. "I guess so. I'm still not sure what we're going to be able to do when he gets here, but at least we can see if he's okay. Just watch out for the propeller."

She started down the rungs, then paused and clung to the railing while she pulled her Keds off. Then she carefully went down step-by-step until her feet were in the water. "Good thing I wore shorts!" she called back up at them.

Holding tight onto the ladder's metal rail, she lowered herself until the water came above her knees. She swished one leg then the other around in the river. "Yikes, cold! Any idea how long this takes?" Her teeth chattered within a few minutes.

Rob pointed upriver. "Look! What's that? Is that like what we saw from the boat, Jane?"

She turned and saw the familiar V-shaped wake approaching. She took a deep breath, then sat down on the ladder, her back to the boat, and her feet still in the water. She kicked her feet as if she were in a swim class learning the flutter kick.

"Yep, here he comes. I haven't seen him in a while. It looks like he's gotten pretty big." Edward squatted down in the cabin, holding onto the ladder rail.

Rob crouched on the other side. "Dang, I didn't get a good look at him the other day. Look at that!"

Jane looked up and saw her brother pointing, his eyes wide. She followed his indication and saw a round shape breaking the surface at the front of the disturbance. The tail flicked out of the water some thirty feet behind it.

It approached within five or six feet of her, then stopped and rose out of the water. She stared into bright blue eyes that matched her own and her brother's — but these were the eyes of a very old soul. The two regarded each other for a long beat.

Jane realized she was holding her breath.

"Douglas? Can you hear me?" their father called from the cockpit behind her.

The creature broke eye contact with Jane, looking up at the man. The head moved up and down.

"I've explained to the children what our family is all about, Douglas. They understand about the changing. And how you need Emily to change you back."

The head dropped down a moment, then lifted again and stared at Jane. It bobbed up and down twice.

Edward shrugged. "Okay, he understands. That's about as much as I've ever been able to talk to him, though. Jane, do you want to try?"

Jane pondered a moment, then leaned forward a bit. "Grandpa? Grandpa Douglas? Hi, it's… it's Jane. I don't think you've seen me since I was little. I'm almost grown now. I miss you…"

The creature that was her grandfather moved a bit closer. Jane sat quietly as it came within a few feet of her, then held out her hand to it. It came closer and touched her hand with its head.

"Dad, it's not going to bite her, right?" Rob spoke quietly to their father, who shook his head and held a finger to his lips.

The serpentine face nuzzled her hand. Jane held perfectly still for a moment, then slowly stroked the top of the creature's head, and he pushed against her knee with the side of his face, rubbing up and down.

"Wow, he's never let me touch him in all these years. I think he recognizes the family blood connection, hon." Edward spoke quietly. "Just no sudden moves, okay, sweetie?"

She nodded, mesmerized by the connection she felt with the strange creature in front of her. "I'm sorry, Grandpa. I'm sorry that Grandma isn't here anymore. Do you remember? I'm so sorry. I'm sure you've been looking for her all these years, haven't you?" She stroked the top of the head and rubbed between his eyes.

The creature came closer and nuzzled his head between her arms. After half a beat, she let go of the railing and hugged around his neck.

Suddenly, the creature reared its head back, giving her a wide-eyed stare. The massive body thrashed in the water, making giant waves leap up in a roiling mass that rocked the boat.

The creature spun in the water and slammed against the stern of the boat. Rob yelled, "Look out!"

Jane grabbed for the railing of the ladder but missed—and screamed as she pitched forward into the maelstrom.

Chapter Seventeen

Edward lunged forward and grabbed ahold of the back of Jane's life vest, pulling her back to the ladder. She managed to grab the railing and clung there, shaking, for a long moment.

She looked back up at her father. "I... I don't know why he did that. It seemed like he was happy to see me, and then... did I do something wrong?"

"No, hon. It did seem like he was happy, but then when his face got up close —"

"I bet he thought you were Grandma." Ron interrupted his father. "Then when he got close enough —"

Edward struck his forehead with the heel of his hand. "Yes! He figured out you weren't Grandma even though you smelled like her, and he got confused. Jane, are you okay?"

She gave a little smile, still clutching the ladder railing with both hands in a white-knuckle grip. "Um, yes? I think so. What's he doing? Where did he go?" She turned and looked across the water. Fifty yards behind them, the waves in the water formed a circle, but it calmed even as they watched.

"Come on in now, hon. I'm not willing to risk losing you too." Edward held out his hand to her.

She frowned and shook her head, turning back to the water. "No, I think he's calming down."

"Look!" Rob pointed to where the whirling circle had been. The water had quieted, and the familiar V-shape slowly moved toward them. "He's coming back!"

Jane spoke quietly as she watched the water. "I want to try again, Dad. We can't leave him out here forever, and we may never get another chance. We don't have Mom anymore, and he's... he's *family*."

Edward sighed. "All right, let's at least see what he's going to do. But be ready for anything, and don't let go of the ladder." He grabbed the back of her life vest again.

Rob stepped to the cabin and returned with the boat hook from the roof. "Just in case."

Jane moved lower down the ladder, putting her legs in and waving one hand back and forth in the water while holding the ladder with the other. "Grandpa? Douglas?"

The creature's head rose out of the water a few feet away, eying them without coming any closer.

Jane held out her arms. "I love you, Grandpa. Can you come back to us? Can you come back to being a person? Or… or have you been in there too long?"

Edward leaned forward and spoke quietly to her. "Tell him this, Jane. Say, 'Come back to me, come back from the sea. Come back to me, our love will always be.' That's what Grandma used to say to call him back. I've tried saying it myself, but… I don't have the family power since I only married in. And of course, I'm a man." He stumbled on the last words.

The creature came closer and rested its head on her knee. Jane stroked his head and repeated the words.

A tremor ran through the sea creature, and after a moment, he backed up out of her arms, swimming away into the water, then came toward her again, stopping a few feet away.

She repeated the words. He circled slowly, coming to her, again and again, several times as she repeated the calling. "Come back to me, come back from the sea. Come back to me, our love will always be."

On the fourth round, she noticed a change in the face. It seemed to morph, changing before her very eyes, and she held her breath. The two long, fluid arms that sloped away from the narrow shoulders reached up and gripped the railing of the ladder on either side of her. The entire part of the body above the water spasmed, splashing her. And then the back end of the creature thrashed in the water.

Jane clung to the ladder railing and felt her father's fingers tighten on the back of her life vest. It reassured her that she wasn't going to get dragged into the whirlpool that again formed before her.

The head ducked under the water as the features started flowing together, and she saw it shake violently. Then all was still for a moment.

The top of the head rising out of the water in front of her now sprouted long tendrils of dark hair streaked with gray that swirled in the water as he brought his face up into the air and cast a shuddering breath. She looked into his face—the face of her grandfather.

"Grandpa! It's you. You're back!"

She wrapped her arms around him and pulled him closer to the ladder. "Hold on, hold on!"

The old man clung to one side of the ladder. Jane's father pulled her up the steps into the boat, then went down the rungs and helped the older man. Rob grabbed a large beach towel from the bag and wrapped it around his grandfather as he stood there shivering and naked in the boat.

Jane turned away while they helped him dress in the green plaid shirt and green pants that Edward had brought. The boat had drifted back toward the marina while they were occupied. She peered at the dock but saw no sign of the attendant.

The four of them sat down in the warm sunshine on the floor of the boat, where they were protected from the wind—and from prying eyes.

Jane fished some cheese and crackers out of the duffel bag and passed them to her grandfather. "Are you hungry? I don't know, do you think you still like people food?"

The old man coughed into his hand for a moment, then smiled. "I'll tell you one thing. I think I'm pretty much done with eating fish for the rest of my life. Cheese and crackers would be delightful."

Edward pulled a thermos of coffee out of his duffel bag and chuckled at the look on his father-in-law's face when he opened the top and poured some into the cup on the lid.

"Son, I haven't smelled anything so good in… seriously, I don't know how long. How long has it been?" The older man took the steaming plastic cup from his son-in-law's hands and sipped, then put it on the deck.

Edward reached out and took both of Douglas's hands. "I have some feeling as to how different it is when you're underwater, Douglas. I remember that the only thing saving my sanity was having Rachel call me back… back onto the shore and back to being a person. I've tried to call you back for a long time now, but…"

He looked at his children, then at their grandfather. "Even though Rachel extended the talent to me, and that let me swim in the water with you, I wasn't born with it. I don't have the talent myself."

He heaved a big sigh. "But, that was a long time ago. It may not have seemed it to you, but as you can see, the twins are almost adults now. I'm sorry, Douglas, but it's been ten years that you've been in the water as Bessie."

The old man's hands shook in his son-in-law's grasp. "Ten years?" he whispered. "How… how could she leave me in there that long? *Why didn't Emily call me back?*"

"Oh, Grandpa," Jane said and threw her arms around his shoulders.

He leaned into her and smiled, then pulled one hand away from Edward to smooth her hair. "I'm sorry about scaring everyone. You look like my Emily when we first fell in love."

A sob escaped Jane's lips.

Her grandfather patted her cheek. "Is that how you called me back, dear? Thank you."

She smiled at him through her tears. As she sat back, he put an arm around her.

The older man looked back to his son-in-law. "I don't have a good feeling about this. Tell me straight out. Why didn't Emily call me back?"

"The boat accident," Edward said. "The last time you saw her, remember?"

The old man nodded slowly.

Edward went on. "The women made me take the children to shore. When I came back, my wife… your daughter, Rachel… turned me back, but she drowned. The Marine Unit looked, they looked for days, but they never found Emily."

"What do you mean they didn't find her? Where was she?" The old man shook his head as if to clear a fog.

"I think she drowned too, Douglas. That's the only explanation I have for why she hasn't returned. Why she didn't come back to you." He looked down, then back up at the older man. "For why she didn't call you back to yourself. She must've drowned in the accident, and they never found her body."

Douglas's eyes were wide and brimming with tears. "No. No, you think she's dead? But… but I just saw her. I swear, I just saw her on the boat. I remember. She was wearing a red-and-white striped dress."

"Grandpa, that was ten years ago." Rob reached out and gripped his grandfather's hand. "I remember it a little bit, and I was just a little boy. But look at us now. I'm taller than my dad."

The older man seemed to shrink in upon himself. His chest fell, and his head drooped. "I've been searching, searching for so long. I had no sense of time. Then I thought I caught a scent of her. Just the other day. Was it her?" He looked at Jane. "Or was it you?"

She nodded. "Rob and I went out on a boat for the first time in ten years. I trailed my fingers in the water, and you came to us right away. It was a little scary, but now I understand. You weren't trying to hurt us or scare us. You were just looking for Grandma. For your wife."

The old man looked down at himself. He held out his wrinkled arms and examined them. "So, I'm back in my human body. I could... stay with you all. I could, right?" He looked up at them, and the other three nodded and smiled.

"Oh yes, Grandpa! Please, come home and live with us," Jane said.

Rob and Edward nodded.

Edward leaned toward him. "There's always a place for you with us, Douglas. You're family. We're family."

Douglas stared at the floor of the boat for a long time, then raised his head and looked out at the water. "I don't know where I belong anymore. You are all family, of course. But" — his breath caught for a moment before he went on — "but you're not my Emily. And from what you say, she's in there somewhere. I've always had the sense that she was near." He gestured at the water with his chin, watching the current coursing downstream.

He sat back from the other three and paused for a moment. "And that's where I belong too. With my Emily. I love you all, but I need to be with her. We had an agreement to love each other forever. And never forget the other."

With those words, he leaped to his feet with a nimbleness that Jane had not expected and jumped onto the gunwale of the boat. He dove off the side, making a beautiful arc against the sky as he hung in the air for a moment, then hit the water and submerged with a graceful fluid motion.

"Grandpa!" Jane jumped up and tried to go after him, but her father grabbed her arm.

"Wait, hon. We can't help him. And he can't change to Bessie without your grandmother."

Rob jumped up, and the twins wrapped their arms around each other as they watched the spot where their grandfather had gone under the water. Jane's eyes tracked downriver, and she saw his head break the surface for a moment, far downstream where he got caught by the current heading around the east side of the next island — toward the construction site above the Falls. Submerged a second time.

They did not see him come up again.

CHAPTER EIGHTEEN

The authorities met them at the dock when they returned to the marina. The attendant had apparently woken up just as Douglas dove off the boat, and he put in a panicked call about seeing a man falling overboard. Edward talked to them after they docked the boat, protecting the twins from having to say anything, and dropped them off at home before going into work.

He told them they didn't have to go to school the next day but that he would call when he could. He apologized that the dam project was at a critical phase and hugged them both a long time before leaving, and they reassured him they would be all right.

When they got inside, Rob disappeared into his room and started his music. Jane heard Bob Dylan throbbing away through his floor.

She sat in her reading chair, holding the diary but not opening it. She felt numb when she thought about her grandfather going back in the water because he couldn't be with the woman he loved on land. Or because he wanted to be with the woman he loved in the water. And wondered if she'd ever experience a feeling that strong.

Her thoughts went to all the times her family had spent together when she was little. One time they were picnicking on the grounds at Niagara Falls, each consuming a whole quarter of a small watermelon for dessert with a knife and fork; she'd eaten the middle of the wedge of juicy red fruit, leaving the juice contained by a thin layer around the edge. She'd cried when Rob had reached out with his fork and broke the thin layer of red fruit holding all the juice in, and it had spilled out—but then she was delighted when he said they'd made their own waterfall!

Jane thought back to being tiny and holding her grandfather's hand on the *Maid of the Mist* boat tour—how they'd gotten so close to the bottom of the Falls that she had laughed in delight when she felt the droplets of water on her face. She could almost hear the roar and feel the vibrations in her bones. How could they possibly turn off all that water?

And, she mused, it would be an astounding thing to see the rock underneath the Falls with no water. She wished she could stand at the bottom and look up.

Later in the afternoon, she went out to the rock garden in the back yard and picked a little bouquet of the blue forget-me-nots that had grown out there ever since she could remember, brought them in, and put them in a glass of water on the kitchen counter. She looked at them for a long time, thinking about the stories in the diary.

"I miss you, Mom. Grandma. Grandpa." She finally allowed herself to cry.

Brother and sister sat together and talked later that evening before turning in for the night. About family. About love. About what it meant to be a human being. Then they each collapsed into their beds.

The best Jane could tell the next day was that their father hadn't been home all night—and she hoped that meant the dam project was going well. She started looking through the old family scrapbooks her mother had kept of their childhood and adding some of the pictures she'd taken recently, including their trip on the boat.

Their father called mid-morning to tell them that the water over the Falls had indeed been stopped. Jane congratulated him, then frowned when he suggested they leave the TV off. She agreed but was so distracted by the scrapbooks that she promptly forgot.

When *Dark Shadows* came on after school, she and Marilyn talked on the phone together while they watched, and that made her feel better.

That night at dinner, the two siblings were eating hotdogs and salad—at least it was easy to cook—while the TV kept its constant stream of commentary that they usually didn't notice.

Jane's ears perked up at some of the words, though, and she turned to look over her shoulder at it. "Turn it up!"

"Look!" Rob reached over and adjusted the volume on the TV. "It's the report about the Falls. Look at that!"

The pair gaped at the small television on the counter. The footage had been taken by helicopter as it flew down the Niagara River toward the Falls, showing the rushing water underneath. It still seemed to have the same amount of current and waves as usual, but when it got to the large dam that jutted out from the shore and across the branch of the river, the water diverted to the left.

The helicopter continued past the dam showing the dry rock bed of the river, with a few small pools of water trapped in crevices in the rock, and then—it went over the top of where the Falls should be. The two saw the ground drop away from beneath the helicopter camera in a sudden change that made Jane's heart lurch.

Far below the helicopter, the jagged chunks of rock that had crumbled off the Falls over the years lay stacked upon each other. They could see workers in bright yellow vests, moving below like ants on an anthill, making their way from point to point through the talus and examining the rock.

The voiceover explained that the workers were examining the rock face to see if they could stabilize it. The hope was that the rock talus at the bottom could be removed to restore the full depth that the water dropped and make the Falls look more majestic.

"Hey, kids, I'm home!" Their father's voice sounded tired as he came through the back door.

"Oh, Dad, so glad to see you. Look, it's on TV!" Jane beamed at him, holding one finger up to her lips.

"Oh no, I wanted to tell you myself—"

Rob shushed him, eyes glued to the screen. Edward came to stand between his two children and placed a hand lightly on each one's shoulders.

The film cut away to an interview with a geologist, who explained that it seemed as though the giant rocks at the bottom were supporting the rock that formed the Falls. He appeared crestfallen and said that it was not likely they would be able to remove those giant boulders. But they could do some work on the top—the lip where the water went over—and secure the rock more tightly to prevent any more from crumbling over the edge and eroding the Falls.

The interviewer asked him, "Is it true what we've heard, that the workers have made some grim discoveries?"

The camera closed in on the geologist's face again. His features drooped, and he firmed his lips for a moment before answering. "Yes, I regret that we have found the bodies of two people at the bottom of the Falls. One is a man dressed in green clothing, who is likely the individual reported to have gone into the water yesterday. I'm sorry to say that he did not survive his trip over the Falls."

"Oh no!" Jane cried. "Grandpa!"

"Is that all?" the reporter asked, then put the microphone back to the geologist.

He shook his head. "No, we found another body that had been there much longer, that of a woman in a red-and-white striped dress. I don't believe we will be able to identify who she is from her appearance, as it's been too long. But she was wearing what appears to be a wedding ring on her left hand, a small gold band with some engraving inside."

Jane grabbed Rob's arm.

They both leaned in so as not to miss his words.

The geologist went on. "We found the words, 'Forget Me Not' engraved inside the ring."

Author's Note

This tale is based upon news stories that a carnival on the south shore of Lake Erie used reports of Bessie the sea monster to draw crowds to their show in the 1930s.

Likewise, the actions of stopping the water over the American side of Niagara Falls on Thursday, June 12, 1969, by building a cofferdam are all based on fact.

When they stopped the water, they did indeed find two bodies. One was a man in green pants and a green plaid shirt who was presumed to have been the man who was seen going into the water the day before.

The other was a woman in a red-and-white striped dress who had been under the water long enough that she could not be identified — save for her wedding ring with the inscription 'Forget Me Not' inside.

ABOUT THE AUTHOR

Carol Gyzander writes and edits horror, dark fiction, and science fiction. Her stories are in over a dozen anthologies, including a dark fantasy story, "Deal With the Devil" in the alternative Beatles anthology, *Across the Universe: Tales of Alternative Beatles*, edited by Michael Ventrella and Randee Dawn.

Her Bram Stoker Award-nominated story "The Yellow Crown" is in *Under Twin Suns: Alternate Histories of the Yellow Sign*, from Hippocampus Press. This weird historical fiction anthology, edited by James Chambers, explores the madness of Robert W. Chambers' classic work of weird fiction, *The King in Yellow* (1895) and those under the sway of the Yellow Sign.

She's the Editor of Writerpunk Press, where she's edited four charity anthologies of punk stories inspired by Poe and classic horror. Their latest anthology is *Taught by Time: Myth Goes Punk*.

Carol is Co-Coordinator of the Horror Writers Association (HWA) NY Chapter and one of the co-hosts of the monthly HWA NY Galactic Terrors online reading series. As HWA Chapter Program Co-Manager, she helps support chapters in the US.

HWA, MWA, SinC. Find her at CarolGyzander.com, or on Twitter and Instagram @CarolGyzander.

artist's rendition of Bessie, The Lake Erie Monster

BESSIE
THE LAKE ERIE MONSTER

(Also referred to as South Bay Bessie, The Lake Erie Monster, Great Snake of Lake Erie, and Knock-off Nessie)

ORIGINS: A regional cryptid similar to the Loch Ness Monster, also referred to as Nessie, and Champy of Lake Champlain's fame, Bessie is said to inhabit Lake Erie, which borders on New York, Pennsylvania, Ohio, Michigan, and Canada. There have been documented sightings up and down the coast for over one hundred and thirty years.

However, legends of a lake monster in the area predate these recorded cases. Tribes in the region, particularly the Iroquois, have long told tales of Oniare, a horned dragon-like snake that also calls the Great Lakes home.

Though sharing the singular moniker of Bessie, some believe there to be a population of these creatures living in the lake, which supports the highest fish production in the Great Lakes. This would account the scope and variations of the reportings.

DESCRIPTION: Generally cited as a long, snake-like creature averaging about one to two feet in diameter (though some accounts have reported as much as four) and between fifteen and sixty feet long. Bessie is said to have four flippers and a flat tail, but accounts vary as to whether her head is shaped like a dog's, snake's, or horse's.

There is also some variation in reported coloration, ranging from silver or grey, to copper-like, to greenish-brown or black.

Several accounts describe the creature's body as cigar-or sturgeon-shaped and reptilian, and some even claim the creature has arms.

The scientific community have proposed several possible explanations for the reported activity, including a population of creatures related to either the Plesiosaur or Ichthyosaurus, or in the case of the swimmers inexplicably bitten, Blowfin, a species of highly agressive, prehistoric-looking fish with strong jaws and well-developed teeth.

LIFE CYCLE: Unknown, though it is theorized that several unexplained attacks on swimmers in Lake Erie could be the result of young Bessies learning how to feed.

HISTORY: The first sighting of a Bessie was reported in 1793, near Sandusky, Ohio. The captain of the sloop *Felicity* startled the creature when shooting at some ducks. Several more incidence occured on the waters, with some of the sailors firing muskets on the creature, to no effect.

In 1817, two French brothers happened about a Bessie apparently in its death throes. They fled at the sight, but later returned only to find the remains swept out to sea in their absence, leaving behind only sand disturbed by the creature's thrashing and a handful of silvery scales the size of a half-dollar.

Several witnesses over the years have spied this cryptid jumping about in the waters of the lake, either in seeming combat with some unseen creature below, or playfully.

Bessies do not seem to have a fear of humans, with many reports of them coming quite close to observers, sometimes agressively, other times not.

The natives of the region have embraced their local legend, honoring it in the naming of their sports teams and even their microbrews. Bessie has even been immortalized in road-side sculptures and made cameos in children's cartoons.

Not everyone, however, seems quite enamored with the Lake Erie Monster. There are reports of a local marina offering a $100,000 reward for Bessie... dead or alive.

Although Jason Whitley has worn many creative hats, he is at heart a traditional illustrator and painter. With author James Chambers, Jason collaborates and illustrates the sometimes-prose, sometimes graphic novel, *The Midnight Hour,* which is being collected into one volume by eSpec Books. His and Scott Eckelaert's newspaper comic strip, Sea Urchins, has been collected into four volumes. Along with eSpec Books' Systema Paradoxa series, Jason is working on a crime noir graphic novel. His portrait of Charlotte Hawkins Brown is on display in the Charlotte Hawkins Brown Museum.

CAPTURE THE CRYPTIDS!

Cryptid Crate is a monthly subscription box filled with various cryptozoology and paranormal themed items to wear, display and collect. Expect a carefully curated box filled with creeptastic pieces from indie makers and artisans pertaining to bigfoot, sasquatch, UFOs, ghosts, and other cryptid and mysterious creatures (apparel, decor, media, etc).

http://CryptidCrate.com

www.ingramcontent.com/pod-product-compliance
Lightning Source LLC
Chambersburg PA
CBHW031031190726
48286CB00003BA/1121